CW01096092

Tilting At The Darkness

Leslie P Garcia

Published by Leslie P Garcia, 2024.

TILTING AT THE DARKNESS

First edition. October 22, 2024.

Copyright © 2024 Leslie P Garcia.

ISBN: 979-8227515070

Written by Leslie P Garcia.

Table of Contents

Only Words

It's only words, and words are all I have
To take your heart away. –**Bee Gees**

Like many, perhaps most, writers, words are such a constant passion in my life that they sometimes consume me. The right word is essential to convey even the most trivial social media update. Text messages to my kids and grandkids, Facebook posts—days after I send them, I reread them and correct them if need be.

I could blame it on Shakespeare's admonition that "the pen is mightier than the sword." I could blame it on my childhood in a dysfunctional family in which the most important topic of the day was some college-level word from a book by the conservative Yale graduate William F. Buckley. The truth may be simpler than that—in an abusive household where ridicule and high academic were everything, and normalcy and safety were nothing—I could control words. And I just always read—always.

My early writing caught the attention of my principal—she posted my first story on the bulletin board. *Ricky and Tricky's Christmas*. A poem—the worst poem in the world, I'm sure, because I can't rhyme poetry in a meaningful way—was published by a short-lived magazine called *Kids*, written entirely by kids.

Emboldened by such a quick, positive result, I knew I'd be a best-selling author by second or third grade. I mean, I'd received a dollar and fifty cents for a poem before I was seven.

No matter how good your words are at six—you need to live them, cherish and build on them a little more. By third grade I was punished—severely—for the words my father found in my pants' pocket. Words to advice columnist Dear Abby, asking help not for myself and my siblings, but for my mother. The words must have been powerful—they touched off a nightmare.

After that, I still wrote, but most of what I wrote went unread. Just words.

I did write a western comedy romance for John Wayne, Dean Martin and my sister's crush Ed Martin to star in. My sister and college friend loved it, but John Wayne, Dean Martin and Ed Martin never got to see it. My father burned it when, after moving to the Texas hill country, an undocumented migrant worker on a dude ranch asked for my hand. In Spanish.

Word is, we Cancers are notorious homebodies. Family is everything. I believed that even before I read Debra Dixon's book on sun signs.

So, after disowning me, beating me one more time, and telling my family to keep away from me, the man who drilled my siblings and me in vocabulary, history and math did the worst thing he could have—he burned *Preach*, my John Wayne book. Three hundred hand-written pages. Each word carefully chosen and evaluated while others in my chemistry class bored themselves with the periodic table and such.

Not to be blasé about the destruction losing even a dysfunctional family causes, but losing those words crippled me for years. I accumulated rejection letters—hundreds of them—at a period when just paying postage for an envelope and an SASE (self-addressed stamped envelope) was a burden. Had children who held life my life together, worked, went to college. I wrote—writers do that. But I also doubted that any word I put down on paper would ever really matter.

Fortunately, I also learned new words. Spanish, from television programs and from singers I had crushes on. Those words helped me find sanity again. With two languages and a whole new culture to explore, I wrote at one or two in the morning. (That's what moms attending college, working and raising children do, right?)

On December 9th, 2012, I got an email—no more SASEs—from new romance publisher Crimson Romance. "Wow," it said. "Unattainable blew me away." There was an attachment—the manuscript back, I knew. Editors always returned unwanted manuscripts back then.

I pounded my desk. I cried. I cursed, which I seldom do. I thought I would die.

And then I asked myself—if I blew her away, why did she return it? So, I opened the email again and looked at the attachment. It was a contract.

I shook. I walked down the long hall crying so hard I could hardly walk.

The first person I ran into was my oldest granddaughter—and she was the first to find out that the words finally worked.

My grandkids warn me against turning everything into a life lesson, so I'll just offer some writerly advice—don't ever give up on *your* words. Every novel, every poem, even every song lyric, is born from words. If you never sell a piece of writing, or share it, or even finish it—part of your heart is in the words you choose, the words that are your voice.

"It's only words?" Dear Bee Gees, you got it wrong. It's **all** words.

***

This Writer's Very Early Life

These days, I can forget what I'm saying while I'm saying it—yet I have remarkably clear memories from the past. At least I think I do. One of the beauties of being a grandma is that you're two generations removed from your own parents, so no one can argue that any of your memories are wrong.

One of the memories that my older sister Stephanie and I share is paddling around in the orange life jackets in the Pacific Ocean next to Roy Rogers' yacht. Apparently, we had a boat somewhere along the same dock, but I don't remember ours. I don't really remember the yacht, except that it was huge, and there was a monkey that ran around loose. Stephanie and I chased it and got lost. I suppose if we were on the yacht, we met Roy, too, but he didn't become important until I fell in love with Trigger.

One of the clearest memories I have is that I should have died when I was four. Shortly after we left once beautiful California for Texas, I took a header off a 7-foot corral fence, landing on the top of my head, and blacking out.

My mom and dad didn't take me to the doctor, but for 12 hours they made me drink coffee to be sure I stayed awake in case of a concussion. I'm a little surprised now that that much coffee didn't kill me, and I've been an insomniac all my life—but I haven't drunk coffee since.

Only recently have I started to wonder what The Fall may have changed. How is it possible that such a hard impact had no effect on my brain? Fortunately, it didn't keep me from reading at 5—Jane and Dick books did work, guys—and writing.

The principal at whatever school in Texas I attended posted my first ever story—written in Kinder—on the bulletin board, and just that early I decided I loved to write. The story—one of those details I talked about remembering—was "Ricky and Tricky's Christmas." Two bunnies gave each other gifts. Not a great story, or particularly original—but someone read it!

By first grade, I was unstoppable, and my sister Stephanie had also begun writing. We both had our first sales at the same time to a quickly defunct magazine called *Kids*. $1.50 each, for her article and my awful rhyming poem. But that pushed us both into the belief that writing mattered more than anything, and our writing careers were born.

We had no clue that writing became more complicated and less lucrative after those first sales.

Like so many others literary figures, we were washed up by second and fourth grade.

And so, we did what writers do—we wrote anyway. At the time, we didn't realize that writing is its own reward.

(We didn't really learn that for a while, but it sounds better than "we cried as we wrote our next rejection-to-be.)

When you write, words eventually find you.

***

La Llorona

Electronic candles flickered and wavered against the back wall of the tent, creating an atmosphere of suspense. Or danger.

The three six-year-olds sat surrounded by stuffed animals and princess-themed bedding, giggling and enjoying their own silly jokes.

"We should tell scary stories," Reyna suggested. "Daddy says when you camp out, you tell scary stories."

"What kind of scary stories?" What kind of scary stories?" Melissa sounded hopeful. "Like the good witch in *la pelicula*—"

"Talk English," Reyna countered, with grade school superiority. "The movie. The one with Dorothy."

The third girl, smaller and quieter than her friends, pushed dark curls from her pale face. "The Wizard of Oz isn't scary. Not really."

"We're in first grade." Reyna gave an exaggerated shrug, a cute one like the kids on the sitcoms she watched. She lifted her hands in mock exasperation, palms up, toward Becky. "So, what's scary?"

"*La Llorona*—the ghost mother."

Melissa added an over-stuffed turtle to the collection of stuffed animals in her death grip and moved closer to Reyna. And farther away from Becky.

"G-ghost mother?" she asked.

Becky nodded somberly. "They say she put kids in the river. Drownded them."

"Why?"

Becky's thin shoulders hunched. "It's why she's always crying, though. Why they say she's the crying woman—"

"My mom told me this story once," Reyna interrupted. "She called her the weeping woman." Reyna's eyes grew intent as she remembered. She pointed at Becky "*La Llorona*—like your mother—"

Becky looked around the tent, her eyes a little wild, her gaze skittering like candlelight. Then she faced her friends. Her body stilled and her eyes went hard.

"Yes," she said. "Like my mother." Then she smiled and reached out to touch Melissa. "But it's okay. She won't come back. Not tonight."

Wind whispered and rustled in the mesquite trees and through the reeds reaching down to the water's dark edge. Alejandra Ortega drew a deep breath and looked around. Nothing moved in the darkness but sweat broke out on her forehead and arms. She forced herself on, careful not to slide down the steep, slippery outcropping that disappeared abruptly into the Rio Grande's flood swollen waters.

The rock closest to the water was large and reasonably flat; Alejandra paused there, tensing as she cast another glance around. "Silly!" she scolded herself. The dangers here were very real—drug smugglers. *Coyotes*, or alien smugglers. Men who wouldn't hesitate to rape, kill. Sometimes the river yielded up its victims. Sometimes it didn't.

And here she was, looking for a ghost. Afraid, for God's sake, of finding a ghost. A shudder shook her hard, and she almost slipped into the water.

Dear Lord, was she crazy?

Her husband thought so. Jim was supportive and undemanding—usually. But he had ridiculed her interest in *La Llorona*, the fabled "wailing woman" of Mexican folklore, for weeks now. Good thing business had spirited him away. If he weren't in Dallas, he would be here. And if he were here, well—he wouldn't have approved of his wife and the mother of his child traipsing around a lonely riverbank near midnight.

The wind shifted, changed subtly. Became more a moan than a steady breath of air moving across the river. Chilled her.

Legend said that, more than a hundred years ago, the area's wealthiest rancher set his eyes on a beautiful, but destitute, young woman. Over the objections of family and friends, the man moved into her hutch along the river, insisting that he would live with her in poverty rather than betray his love for her.

And then—he left. To marry a woman of prestige and money. A woman of his own class, whose children he would claim proudly.

Alejandra shut her eyes, tried to block out the surreal images that assaulted her. This was what no one understood. Everyone here had grown up with the legend. Parents passed it on to children, to scare, to amuse, to preserve culture and tradition. To them, *La Llorona* represented nothing more than a scary story on a steamy night, a ghostly figure that haunted the riverbanks in fiction, but not in fact.

But she felt the legend, lived it, knew what happened.

Faced with abandonment, the woman snapped. Her harshest critics said that she simply sought revenge. He could have married her, given the children a name and his money, but after using her, he had tossed her away. Sad, but there you are. *Hell hath no fury*, and so the woman had drowned her babies to avenge her betrayal. As if, they pointed out, he cared—other children would come. And those children he would honor and love. But her children were lost forever—gone in a jealous rage.

The others, kinder souls who had drawn strength from their own suffering, but not despair, said that the woman couldn't bear seeing her little ones suffer the poverty and hunger of her own childhood. In a time when the sins of the flesh were condemned, no one came forward to help. Without hope for the wellbeing of those she loved most, she committed a sacrifice born of love.

A sob tore from Alejandra's throat as the distraught young woman brought her children to the river's dark banks. The river raged that night, swollen by recent rains. Not unlike the dark, rushing water this very night. The children were so tiny, so trusting. One by one, they were delivered into the river's black, black depths.

Tears streamed down Alejandra's cheeks, hot and wet even in the summer heat.

The wind picked up, wailed around her, although the trees and bushes had gone completely still.

"*¡Mis hijos! ¡Mis hijos!*" Was it the wind, or the woman wailing into the night, searching for her children as she realized what she had done? Shivering uncontrollably, Alejandra took a step forward and down. The river's dark water covered her feet. She started, jerked away as if she had been shocked. Wading a few steps down along the bank, she found a place where she could scramble out of the water.

Crazy! She was crazy! What had driven her into those waters, polluted with the waste of cities now sprawling along the river's length? She shuddered again, wiped a hand across her bare forearm. Turned surprised eyes down to the slight sheen of wetness. Why were her arms wet?

Hidden somewhere around a curve in the riverbank, the murmur of voices. Spanish-speaking. Probably not Border Patrol then. Undocumented aliens, if she was lucky. They would be less likely to attack than drug runners, especially if they were accompanied by women.

Quietly, with the silent grace of a wraith, she made her way up from the river, back into the dense underbrush. Even if she were seen now, half lost in the wild growth, she would have the same chance of escape as her hunters would have to capture her. The jumbled vegetation favored no human. Afraid only that her pounding heart could be heard over the night sounds, she made her way slowly, cautiously, but resolutely back to the path that led up to the nature trails behind the community college.

It was funny, she realized, how close the wilderness such as it was now, came to civilization. Much of the city lay along the riverbanks of the Rio Grande, separated by the merest curtain of reeds, tangled bushes and stunted trees. No wonder the myths of the past echoed so deeply in the community. By the time she reached the library parking lot, she had talked herself into sanity again.

Hers was the only car left; it sat, small, dark, and reassuring, under a security light near the brick building. She almost ran the last few steps, desperate now to escape whatever momentary craziness, whatever mindless passions had driven her to the river.

The lights blinked twice as she unlocked the door. She reached for the handle, scarcely able to breathe from her panicked flight away from the river.

"Are you all right, Miss? ¿*Está bien*?"

Alejandra stifled a shriek and whirled around. The man looking at her suspiciously was a uniformed guard. She supposed he had good reason to be suspicious.

She managed a slight smile and a swift nod. "Fine. Thanks."

He looked around, clearly distrustful. Expecting her to be accompanied by someone, probably. Not comfortable that she was here alone. "The library closed hours ago," he noted. The statement accused her, but she just shrugged.

"Wasn't at the library," she answered. "I...was out walking. The nature trails."

That got her another thorough once over. The guard's gaze lingered on her disheveled hair, swept over to note her muddied shoes and pants legs. "At this time of night?" he demanded

I was looking for ghosts. For la Llorona. She couldn't voice her thoughts, though, because he'd call the cops. Or the men in white jackets. So, she shifted slightly and tilted her chin up.

"There aren't any hours posted," she answered, not caring that there were. The river was no man's possession. "Besides, I'm working on a story."

He looked slightly relieved. "You're a reporter? Doing another one of those stories on wetbacks?"

She frowned at his derogatory description of undocumented aliens, but he didn't notice.

"I write," she said. That was true at least.

"You reporters do crazy stuff," he told her, scolding now. "Lady, there's beheadings going on a few thousand yards from here. The reporters across promised the cartels not to say diddly about how many bodies litter the streets at any given moment—"

"Thank you," she murmured, because it was easier than anything else. He watched until she slipped in her car and turned the engine on, then continued on his rounds.

"Third Child Disappears." Alejandra stared at the headline in disbelief. The boy staring up at her had dark, laughing eyes and an angel's smile. Large drops of water splattered across the newsprint, and she glanced up at the sky, startled, looking for a passing rain cloud. For long moments, she didn't feel the wetness on her cheeks, didn't realize that the tears were own. Becky's voice called out to her from behind the wrought iron door, and she turned. The toddler was pressing against the iron, her chubby pink hands wrapped around the elaborate curlicues. The scrollwork turned her daughter's laughing face into a jigsaw puzzle, bits of eyes and smile and dimpled cheeks hidden behind stark black lines.

"Coming, sweetie!" Alejandra tucked the paper under her arm and hurried back to the house. To sanity and the safety of walls and loved ones. Sweeping Becky up in her arms, she danced her daughter over to the high chair and sat her down.

Such innocence. She gave Becky cereal and juice. Goodness, sweetness, and light. Unbidden, the image of the little boy on the front page came bac to her. He was about Becky's age, she knew, although she hadn't read the story. That sweet age of smiles and laughter. She turned away from her own child as the tears came again.

"I'm losing it," she murmured under her breath, in anguish. "Over an old wives' tale, a ghost story!" She crushed her cheeks dry with her forearm and checked her newsfeed. Most of, the comments were from friends calling for the filthy bastard murdering innocent children to be found and killed. Fury vibrated through cyberspace.

One of her flip friends had posted a ghostly image. "Maybe it's the *Llorona*," she posted. And then, "Lol. j/k."

None of her friends thought it was funny. She didn't blame them.

Idly she checked for missed calls; there weren't any.

Jim hadn't called for two days. The call before that was brief, more a matter of routine than concern. Alejandra breathed in deeply, exhaled forcefully. Becky giggled and copied the exaggerated burst of air.

The phone rang shortly after Becky finished breakfast. Alejandra's spirits sank further. From the ring tone, it wasn't Jim. She had hoped he would be home today.

A stranger's voice on the other end asked "Mrs. Ortega?"

After a moment's consideration, she gave a short, unseen nod. "Yes."

"This is Lt. Williams with the police department."

"Yes." Again, she only managed one short word of confirmation.

"Listen, I hate to bother you, but I wondered if you could drop by the station sometime today."

The hairs on the back of her neck bristled, prickled. Absently, she rubbed her neck, and turned her shoulders from side to side.

"Why"

She couldn't think of a single sane reason the police would speak to her. The only conceivable reason remained locked in the depths of her mind, surreal visions of a crime committed more than a century ago. The police weren't interested in the legends of the wailing woman. *La Llorona*. They needed to capture the serial killer preying on the city's children now. She shivered.

On the other end, the lieutenant sighed heavily. "We want to question you about the little boy who disappeared yesterday."

The pain from her neck stabbed downwards, stiffening her shoulders. She tensed, stretched more vigorously, then shivered as chills swept over her body, turning the perspiration on her face and arms to a cold, clammy sweat. A death sweat.

"Officer—"She forgot his name, didn't care what his name was. A note of panic crept into her voice.

"Look, it's just a formality, Mrs. Ortega," Lt. Williams assured her. "The thing is, ma'am, we found the little guy." He paused, his voice filling with the bitterness of a man exposed too often to ugliness and death. "Drowned. In the river."

The floor tilted, and Alejandra clasped the edge of Becky's highchair. Her daughter looked up from the cereal, puzzled.

"What could I possibly know?" Alejandra protested, her fingers clutching the phone with one hand, while the fingernails of her other hand dug into the plastic of the baby's chair.

"The security guard at the college reported seeing you come up from the river. He said you were wet and muddy. He wrote down your plates and called us this morning."

"I explained—"

"Yes, yes." Williams' voice turned soothing. "Look, Mrs. Ortega, all I suspect you of is bad judgement—stupidity, frankly, but nothing else. No story is reason enough to risk your life. But we've got three children snatched from their homes. Drowned along the same stretch of river. We have to follow up on everything. You're a reporter. You understand."

Yes. She understood. But would they? She wasn't a reporter. A writer, she'd told the guard. How would city cops react when they found out she was doing research into the *La Llorona* myth? Worse still, what if she admitted that she saw the frail young woman in her mind, watched as she drowned her little ones in the dark, swirling waters.

"Mrs. Ortega?"

"Yes, Lieutenant?" She paused, wished again that Jim had called. "Just let me drop, my baby off at my mom's, and then I'll go by. Okay?"

"Sure. That'll be just fine," he agreed. "I'll expect you soon, then."

She murmured an assent and hung up. Becky banged her cereal bowl on the tray, then reached out, and Alejandra swept her up in a hug. Becky giggled, placing wet kisses on her cheek and blowing bubbles against her skin.

Alejandra managed a single quick kiss as she set her down.

"We're going to Nana's," she told her daughter. "Go get your bag."

Delighted, Becky toddled off down the hall, hurrying on legs that wouldn't move fast enough.

Alejandra stared after her, her chest so tight that she couldn't breathe as a new image assaulted her. Horrible and terrifying, but the thought still came. *What if I'm her? What if I am La Llorona?*

She slumped into the nearest chair, propped her elbows on the table and buried her face in her hands. She trembled so hard the chair shook as *La Llorona* filled her mind once again, making her wraith-like way to the banks of the Rio Grande. Carrying Becky. An agonized shriek tore through her mind, echoing over and over, muffled, kept from reality by the hands clamped hard over her mouth. But the image didn't go away. La Llorona would come for Becky. Alejandra knew that with absolute certainty. But how could she protect her precious child if she herself were evil incarnate?

The interview with the lieutenant was uneventful. Williams was a gruff, kind career cop, and he didn't consider a woman a suspect in a case like this. He cited statistics and profiles, but Alejandra knew that in this Hispanic culture she shared with him, where most children were coddled and loved, he couldn't believe that a woman—a mother, possibly, with her own children—would kill. Not here, he insisted. Okay, maybe an isolated incident. But not a female serial killer targeting babies. The child killings in other places simply couldn't happen here, even in these sick times.

Alejandra struggled to change his opinion, even though she knew in the back of her mind that she could suffer from increased suspicion. Nothing mattered if these deaths could be halted.

But when she tried to make him see her point by bringing up the story of the wailing woman stalking the riverbanks, he scoffed.

"You're telling me a ghost is stealing kids?" he barked.

"No! You're not listening!" Alejandra protested. "Think about the legend. The circumstances. A woman driven over the edge by betrayal. By abandonment. Ask a psychologist. My women's studies professor had a theory—"

"Save me the crap. Nut case professors teaching what anyone already knows. Women's studies! Yeah, that'll explain—"

"But it could," Alejandra insisted. "It could be a woman. These children haven't been taken by a sex offender. Have they?"

Williams didn't answer immediately, just glared at her.

"Were they sexually abused?"

"Why else does a man ever take a kid—if it's not about custody?"

Williams shook his head, jerked a hand across his mouth. "Lots of reasons. Ransom. Just a crazy damn bastard—"

"Women. They lose their minds too. Maybe more than men. Just listen. The legend—*la llorona*—came from truth at some time."

"Two points." He stood, leaned over his desk, and stabbed a short finger at her. "*La Llorona*, who doesn't and never has existed because she's a ghost, for shit's sake, killed her own kids. Lots of mothers have killed their own kids." He'd worked himself into a state, his breath shortening a little as he talked, face gone red. Again, he stabbed a finger at her. "Point two. Some sicko serial killer's drowning kids in the river and you're here wasting my time! Telling me I should be looking for a fuckin' ghost!"

She drew in a deep breath and took a step back. Away from the anger.

He waved at the door. "Thank you, Mrs. Ortega. We'll call you if we need an expert on old ghost stories."

She accepted dismissal. He thought she was crazy, like Jim did. Not, not like Jim. Jim really thought she was crazy. Lt. Williams just had a killer to catch. She might have visions of a wretched woman lowering those little bodies into the water and wailing. But she wasn't a killer. She and Williams were clear on that.

The interview over, Alejandra picked Becky up and went home. Jim hadn't called. She called him, but he didn't pick up. She didn't leave a message. There was an emptiness filling the house when she went in. She stared again at her phone, checked her social media. Nothing. A missing...presence. With sudden, absolute clarity, she knew.

Jim wouldn't be back. She closed her eyes briefly. A woman, red-headed and beautiful, laughed at her. The woman she had once been, she realized, and her chest constricted until breathing hurt.

Becky yawned and squirmed, wanting down. Gently Alejandra carried her to the sofa and propped her up against the pillows.

Before she could turn on the television, the child dozed off again. Grateful for the respite, Alejandra kicked off her shoes and sat down next to her sleeping daughter, letting the realization, the awareness sweep over her. He wasn't coming home. He had betrayed her. Eventually, sleep's comforting forgetfulness dragged her under.

Alejandra woke to a dark house, starting fearfully and looking around immediately for Becky. The toddler was gone. Heaving herself from the couch, she ran through the house, opening doors, looking. She knew Becky was gone, but still she looked. Bedrooms, kitchen, bath. She even stepped into the backyard.

Outside, she paused for a moment, listening. Low, but with increasing pitch, the wail. "¡Mis hijos! ¡Mis hijos!" *My children, my children.*

Quickly but deliberately, she went in. Changed from her jeans and knit top to a peasant blouse and a long, flowing skirt. Changing clothes made no sense. She needed to do it, though. She shook her hair loose around her shoulders. Touched it, just for a second. The once vibrant red locks were now the color of dried wheat. It didn't matter. She looked in the mirror. Wondered fleetingly what Jim's new woman looked like. If he'd marry her. Then she remembered Becky. Picked up her cell phone and her keys and headed toward the river.

She didn't call the lieutenant until she was almost at the river. He couldn't help, but she knew where to look. She moved, she thought, but she knew that reality no longer existed. Some force outside her sphere of comprehension moved her, tormented her, controlled her.

The river rushed into the night; she could hear it and smell it before she broke out into the clearer area along the banks. She found herself several hundred yards downstream from the previous spot. Here a large clay patch provided safe entry to the river. Tufts of worn grass and a solitary cactus poked up around her. The moon was higher and fuller, or some other unearthly source flooded the banks with the silver light all around her.

She waited. The keening sound grew louder. Broke into sobs, then wailed again, calling endlessly for lost children who would never come. Her past fears flared briefly, fled as a wispy figure drifted from the trees toward the water. Carrying her baby. Carrying Becky.

The pale woman weaved erratically, gliding, then jerking brokenly ahead. Light glowed around her, haloed Becky, mercifully asleep in the woman's cold, thin arms. The cold was palpable, reached out across to her from all that distance. Fear for Becky slammed Alejandra's chest, making it hard for her to step forward.

When she did, the ghostly figure stopped, half-turned. A wild apparition, ready to flee, to disappear into darkness, taking Becky with her.

"Wait," Alejandra breathed. The plea whispered out, but the figure hesitated.

"Your children," Alejandra entreated. "Remember? Your children? Save this one. *Por el amor de Dios*—For God's sake—save this child. She took a tentative step forward, then another. And another. Reached out, pushing her hands through the cold wall keeping Becky away from her.

The woman tensed, jerked back, whirled as if to flee.

"¡Tus hijos!" Alejandra hissed. "Your children. Don't lose your child. Save this child."

Startled into wakefulness by something—Alejandra wasn't sure that her words issued out in real speech, because they seemed soundless in the night—Becky's small body convulsed, and her eyes opened.

"¡*Ama!*" she screamed, struggling to reach Alejandra.

The word chilled Alejandra as nothing else had. Becky didn't speak Spanish. Jim had insisted they only speak English at home. For her to cry out "mother" with such terror—such entreaty in her childish voice—Alejandra reeled, as formless as the figure still clutching her child.

"No! No!" she screamed the words into the night. Did Becky look at her and see death? Two ghostly women struggled for one tiny life on the empty banks of the Rio Grande. Two women—and one of them would surrender this new child to the dark, ungiving depths. With one frantic lunge, Alejandra snatched Becky from the woman's cold, lifeless arms. The figure—woman or wraith—moved toward her, hands outstretched, clutching, clawing.

Alejandra whirled toward the river, holding Becky close, hugging her against her chest. The apparition followed, silent in the water, bobbing and stumbling as if a mortal on precarious footing, but not splashing the water. Alejandra's own foot slipped on a rock, and she fell, twisting Becky to the side to shield her, but grasping her with fierce desperation.

The shrill scream of sirens on the college parking lot broke the unnatural stillness of the night. Two ghostly women rose from the river, both fighting the currents buffeting them, reaching for them. Alejandra splashed to the bank, still cradling Becky against her chest. All around a wail, a thousand lost souls lamenting their grief, rose from the river.

Alejandra staggered a few yards up from the river, then fell to her knees. Becky slipped out of her grasp, but the soft, damp clay cushioned her fall. The figure was gone. *La Llorona*. Her wail faded into the night, replaced by the clamor of the police force, border patrol, and sheriff's department as they crashed through the bushes and reeds.

They burst into the open, guns drawn, lights glaring. Someone took Becky; someone else clapped handcuffs on her wrists. Cold, hard metal, but nothing would ever chill her as much again as reaching into the woman's arms to snatch Becky back from death.

Lt. Williams stared at her, bewildered. "Jesus," he muttered. "Christ! You told me! You—" He shook his head. "Why? Found out about your husband? He called us when he couldn't find you at home. But—the s.o.b. screws around, leaves you"—another head shake. "You get a divorce. You cut off his dick. You don't kill kids."

They read her her rights. She thought someone whispered 'crazy' under his breath.

It didn't matter. Not now. Tomorrow she would explain. She wasn't *La Llorona*. Her hands had not fed those innocent lives to the bloody, dark river. She didn't think. She took a deep, shuddering breath and nodded toward the officers outside the cruiser. Around her, along the river, the wind moaned. Softly, softly, the keening began in her head, around her. "My children, my children!"

The words streamed out, mixed into the wind, rose in intensity. By the time they folded her into the patrol car, the wail was a shriek of anguish, of grief for children lost forever. Her children.

Epilogue

The atmosphere in the tent stilled, went heavy. Outside a slight rustle, moving away from the tent toward the west. Toward the river.

Dampness, a cold moistness, seeped into Becky, and she ran a hand down her arm, still more asleep than awake. But she was gaining awareness, an awareness that made her tense and lie without moving for long seconds, listening.

Becky knew without looking that Melissa wasn't next to her any longer. The knowledge pushed her to her feet. She glanced at Reyna, sleeping soundly, her back turned. Unaware. She wished Melissa were still here.

She searched through the jumble of stuffed animals and plucked out her doll, Baby. She'd had the doll with its soft cloth body and newborn face for years. Spotted and damaged, the eyelids still fluttered up revealing bright eyes. The lips smiled a perpetual smile.

Becky clutched the doll to her and crawled out of the tent. Reyna's parents were snoring in the big tent nearby, the moon high and cold above.

She drifted toward the front of the house, the security lights bright in the backyard, dimmed by the old oak trees in the front yard. But she saw the pool, its white walls gleaming with the silver sheen of the moon.

She stopped at its edge, transfixed for a second. Inside the pool, the water looked dark and still.

She hugged Baby to her fiercely for a moment. Then slowly, slowly, she lowered the doll into the pool. Water wet her arms to her elbows, and she blinked and drew away.

On silent feet, Becky padded toward the street, then turned right. Toward the rising sound of a sudden breeze. Toward the river.

What Kind of Shy?

Back in my fabled childhood days, my parents ranked good manners the most essential skill imaginable. I didn't mind; being polite seemed better than being confrontational, forward, or rude.

Then my eight-year-old brother fell into a boat slip at Lake Altoona (in Georgia) and discovered he couldn't really swim. I raced the short way to where my father and mother were entertaining friends and stopped short. Drinks in hand, sitting around the twenty-two-foot cabin cruiser, chatting in the bright sunlight....

You NEVER interrupt an adult. Never. Only spoiled brats do that. So I waited.

Finally, in desperation, I cleared my throat. "Excuse me," I announced, dying over my rudeness and its potential consequences. "But I think Greg is drowning."

My father shook his head. "We're talking. Besides—I taught him to swim."

"But he's under water," I argued, and moved my arms and legs like a turtle swimming along under the surface. "He's kinda doing this."

The adults took off, and saved my brother. Instead of being punished for being rude, I was punished for not interrupting sooner.

Now and then, I retrieve that memory, dust it off, and wonder what, if any, part that episode played in the shyness that haunted me most of my life. Surprisingly, I could function when I had to. I answered questions in class, could give directions, competed and often won in 4-H events. But whenever I could, I'd be in a corner reading, or on a pony reading, or imagining myself far away in a relationship conjured up from a story I had read.

Social? Not me. I had the skills my parents said were important to be successful in social settings, but no desire to interact.

For a long time, I blamed the etiquette drills for my reluctance to shine in public venues.

Notwithstanding, I became a teacher. For many years, I only spoke when spoken to among adults. Didn't use my mentor's first name for 15 years. Fortunately, I've always been able to relate to kids, and was passionate about education. Any shyness aside, I like to believe I excelled.

Horse Vs. Unicorn

—June 3, 1973. We sit on the couch, the man who will become my husband on one end, me on the other. Our job and perhaps our lives are at stake. Two days ago, when I left the dude ranch to visit my mom and brothers, a pile of rubble was burning. Walking past it, I saw pages of manuscripts, books, and my extensive record collection.

Tears streamed down my face as I opened the door. He came out of the shadows, a tall, dark man that my high school friends found attractive. If only they knew. He unleashed the usual verbal assault—I was a whore, stupid, unworthy of living. The words hurt, even after years of torment, but weren't unexpected.

The kick, though—that came out of nowhere, slamming into my stomach, leaving me lying on my back on the living room floor...

The abrupt call to the post snaps me back to the present. Secretariat, aka Big Red, is stepping toward the track.

I glance at Raul. He's looking at me. He wrangles the horses on the dude ranch, washes dishes, cleans rooms—he works all day, every day, for pennies. I suppose I shouldn't be upset that he's not as excited as me about this rich man's sport or the magic that might happen. Secretariat might win the Triple Crown, a feat not done in my lifetime.

The starting gates burst open, and Secretariat, who has come from behind in every race he's ever run, goes straight to the front.

I start screaming advice to the jockey. He's moving too fast; he has a mile and a half to run. He'll fade at the end. No horse can run that distance full out. Raul's expression probably has gone from indifferent to annoyed. Sometimes I get on his nerves, even though we hardly know each other.

For part of the race, Secretariat's main competitor, a horse named Sham, stays with Big Red. Suddenly, there are no other horses on the TV screen—just one is left, still racing full out for the finish line. He crosses it, 31 lengths ahead of the horse behind him.

I thought I'd scream and jump up and down, that I'd celebrate wildly. I sit back down, stunned by the horse's brilliance. I can't remember a time I didn't love horses, especially thoroughbreds. Secretariat racing alone on that small screen will stay with me for a lifetime, I know. I glance over at Raul. He picked up a magazine sometime during the race and is looking at the ads inside—or the models.

Secretariat is in the winner's circle, white carnations draped over his neck. His owner, Penny Chenery Tweedy, the first woman owner I ever saw at a race track, kisses him on the nose.

And as I stand up to go back to work, I realize I just experienced magic. For the last time.

Forty-three years, two kids, five grandkids and 4 Triple Crown winners later, life happens, day by day. Often the days run into each other, unbound by artificial constraints—since I retired two years ago, there are few demands on my time.

Raul's health deteriorated. At the end, he required round-the-clock nursing. I provided that, being, as always, the obedient, solid person in everyone's life. Doing what was expected—what I expected of myself.

Our kids came by more often, sitting briefly with Raul, hugging me. I wondered if they knew I lived for them, and now for their kids. When I judged myself harshly for staying in a marriage most would have left, or for languishing in a life without magic—I could cling to the goodness in kids. Twenty plus years teaching first grade, two adult kids who lived by the rules and were doing better than I had, and a virtual kaleidoscope of grandkids—I felt blessed. All the time.

Raul died on Derby Day—no. He died on his birthday. The first Saturday in May often coincided with his birthday. I missed the Derby for the only time since I was six. We closed ranks around him, assuring him of his place in Heaven, trying to console each other as he lingered on the edge.

At some point, my oldest, Al, left and brought his two daughters to say goodbye, even though the rest of us argued against it.

"They need to say goodbye," my practical son declared. "They'll be okay."

Caitlyn and Andrea left devastated, tears flooding their faces, collapsing against their mother in desolation.

"I love you, Al," I murmured, trying to soften my tone. "But they aren't ready. Not for this. Not for death."

"Caitlyn's going into eighth grade, Ma." He sighed. "Andrea was Pa's favorite." He held up a hand. "You always say you don't have favorites. You know Pa did. He never denied it. What was that saying of his—*que no tengas pelos en la lengua*?" Al shrugged. "Just admit you favor the older grandkids."

Like me, Al's English was better than his Spanish, even though he had grown up surrounded by Raul's native language.

"But Andrea's only nine—she's the youngest. You shouldn't have let her see her grandpa like that." My protest rang hollow—usually, I was using her age against her, reminding anyone who would listen that she was already nine. She was too old for her unicorns, self-centeredness, and willingness to let others do anything complicated for her.

Still, Andi's pained face when she walked away from her grandfather for the last time was a knife in my heart.

Al brought Caitlyn, and my daughter Wynne came with her husband and three boys. The house overflowed with those who worked with Al and Wynne, or who had worked with me. During a lull in those offering their condolences and pausing to pray by the table holding the urn , Al stopped next to me. He'd cried once in high school when his football team lost the third-round playoff in what might have led to a state title. Now his red eyes and tear-streaked face were haunting.

"I couldn't bring Andi," he told me. "She hasn't slept through the night in three days."

I bit back the "I told you she shouldn't see him," and hugged him. "Her cousins are here, and Caitlyn. Maybe seeing everyone here for her grandpa would have made her feel better."

"She was better at home." He looked around the room. "Mary told me to apologize for not coming, but someone had to stay with Andi."

I nodded, not surprised. Mary and I alternately were fine with each other, and at war. Even in those times during my son's marriage when we'd been 'okay,' we hadn't really. But Al never understood what we meant when we talked about each other "having a face," blowing that off as just woman stuff and focusing on coaching high school football.

You shouldn't have taken her to see him right after he died. Tears stung my eyes, and I stumbled away, dodging people reaching out to hug me or halt me, pretending an urgent need to get to the restroom. Inside the small, private space, with the door shut, I leaned against the door and closed my eyes. There was nothing pretty about death. No fantasy or rainbows and glitter. No wonder Andrea had been devastated. So had I. But in the real world, you suck it up and go on. Maybe not at nine, although...I chased the thought away. I was a hell of a lot older than Andrea, and the sight of Raul with a breathing tube in his mouth and his eyes rolling back in his head still made me sick. I breathed a prayer for Andi, and for her mother too. Then I pulled the door open and went back out into the new reality of my life.

***

Wynne's kids and Caitlyn spun around like tops, laughing and singing along to some song I'd never heard, their devices discarded on the couch. Andrea sat alone on the end farthest from her sister and cousins, grimacing in annoyance.

"Aww, Andi, come on!" Caitlyn called. "Have some fun."

"Fun? You wouldn't know fun if it hit you upside the head and smacked yore ass."

Andi recited the rhetoric the way she'd heard it on TV; her delivery was exaggerated and her intonation not her own. How could Al not notice that this 'bright' daughter of his simply memorized everything she heard or saw, but never bothered to apply anything so that the content became her own?

I walked over and sat down near her. "You know, Andi, you and your cousins don't always get to visit. Your aunt Wynne goes on business trips, your dad coaches something all year—why don't you go play?"

She shrugged, pouted a little and reached for the remote. "I'd rather watch TV," she muttered. "But they need to move."

"They're having fun. You watch too much TV anyway." I took the remote away and tossed it over to the other couch. "How has your summer been?"

"Boring." She yawned and stood up, then reached down for her unicorn. "I'm going to go on a unicorn hunt."

"Do you think they'll have unicorns in 5th grade?" I asked, not trying to keep the sarcasm out of my voice.

She didn't notice, though. "Probably. They'll have unicorns when I'm a hundred years old, Grandma." She sounded serious, and her usual attempts to ridicule others tended to be more blatant, so I wondered if she knew that there weren't unicorns now, and there wouldn't be in a hundred years. Imagination was a great thing; a vivid imagination spun stories in heads and created writers and composers and inventors. Not understanding the differences between imagination and fact, reality and fantasy—well, that was what drove folks to drugs. That was what created adults without knowledge or ambition. If the mental lines became too blurred, you got mad men and serial killers.

You got me. The thought slammed into me, but I shoved it aside. Yes, I'd grown up largely without friends. Being socially accepted was a foreign concept—my parents had been Yankees in rural Georgia, where the Civil War still lived in how you were viewed by others.

And, like child predators—monsters not yet identified as such in those 'better' times, my father isolated my siblings and me as much as possible. But even if I seemed strange to myself and others, I always knew unicorns didn't exist. The magic I believed in back then was based in reality—the chance that I'd do something with my life someday.

Andi didn't have a clue that someday she'd need a life.

That hurt me for her. And irritated me. But I went into the kitchen and pulled snacks out for everyone.

What was that phrase people had been using recently? *Not my circus, not my clowns?* I wasn't sure. *Good god.* I was becoming Andrea—everything popping into my head or out of my mouth was a product of the 'entertainment' industry. I slammed the gallon of juice down and called the kids.

Somehow Andrea got there first.

Two nights later when Al showed up at the door without Mary or the girls in tow, I knew something was wrong. He stalked into the kitchen and looked in the pantry for snacks, a lifelong habit of his, then sat down at the table and checked his phone, not really looking at me.

I sighed, got a can of soda, and sat down, too. "So, what is it this time?" I demanded. "Does Mary think I looked at her cross-eyed or something?"

He flushed, but didn't answer immediately, just turned his wedding ring on his finger a few times. Guilt already needled me—Mary wasn't perfect, but he loved her. Raul hadn't been perfect, but we'd managed forty-three years. Maybe I should just accept Mary for who she would always be... .

He looked down at the ring, as if debating something, then looked up at me. And landed a knockout blow. "Ma, Andi wants to know why you hate her."

Fury flamed through me, incinerated me. The mouthful of soda I had taken spewed onto the polished wood table. Anger engulfed me completely.

I never used the f word. "What the fuck are you talking about?" I gritted.

Al shrugged and drew circles on the table with his finger. "She doesn't want to come. Says all you do is scold her. She said you don't treat her like her sister or cousins."

"I treat them as much the same as I can. Al, do you have any idea how spoiled she is? Everything bores her. Everything makes her tired. She doesn't like anything."

"Except unicorns."

He said it seriously, not helping at all with the anger. "Except that. She's an A & B student, Al. But when you ask her anything—anything—that doesn't come off a TV screen or out of a book, she can't tell you. She's lazy and unmotivated, but she's your baby, and you don't see that. You don't worry about that!"

"Lazy? Because she's not as athletic as the others? You told us a million times you weren't athletic."

"I grew up outdoors camping in the woods. Chasing butterflies and horses. I rode. I didn't base my whole world view on what I saw on *I Dream of Jeannie* or unicorns, Al." I shook my head. "We had this fight before, remember? When you were still putting her shoes on and buckling her seat belt in second grade?"

"You could be kinder," he said, stubbornly. There was silence at the table, then he looked across at me. "You could love her."

"I do love her, Al. But—" I stopped, trying to find the right words. "I was a social outcast all my life, I've told you that. I was awkward. I was weird. You know, everyone says to be yourself, but it's not always that simple." Tears welled up in my eyes. How could he think I hated my own granddaughter? I only wanted her to be...to be okay. Do you realize all those things you tell her are so clever, so cute—they're all off a TV screen. *Mijo*, she doesn't know what 'original' means. She 'wants' to be an inventor—but everything comes out of a sitcom. She makes butt jokes and repeats the sex talk crap she hears, and if you ask her—she doesn't know what she's saying or why it matters. She's self-centered. You know how she interrupts every conversation. She always wants to be the center of attention. She and her cousins never get along, because they annoy her. Is she going to do nothing for the rest of her life but watch TV and play with stuffed toys? You can't want that for her—she's better than that!"

He pushed his chair back and stood up. I stayed where I was. "I'm not worried about her," he said. "Why should you be?"

Because I can see through love and recognize the reality, I thought. I'd seen through Raul—the hardness, the deception, the occasional cruelty. He hadn't had magic or known how to encourage. Andi was only about magic and self. I could see them both. I could love them both. I was surprised that Al couldn't.

He came around the table and kissed my cheek. I wrapped my arms around him and hugged him. "Al, I love you. And I love your girls—both of them. If I didn't love Andi, I wouldn't care so much. Help her be—"

I fished for words, and he finished, "—not herself?" The bitterness was clear.

I stepped away and watched him leave. Sometimes not being yourself was better.

The sitcoms Andi watched had me twisting my hands in the fabric covering the sofa cushions. When had TV for nine-year-olds disintegrated into body humor, unsavory characters and constant references to sex with everyone?

She sat there enthralled, laughing hysterically, sometimes even during commercials, and my only consolation was that she probably didn't have a clue about anything she was seeing.

"Your dad should come for you soon," I told her, partly to stop the laughter and partly because I hoped it was true. He, Mary and Caitlyn were out of town—she was competing in an All-Star Softball Tournament, and Andrea had stayed with me for the last two days.

"Yippee!" She fished the battered, stuffed unicorn she took everywhere from between the seat cushions waving it around in crazy arcs. "I'm Magic Angel Unicorn and I'm so happy I'm pooping glitter and rainbows!" she crowed in a falsetto that raised the hair on my arms and stabbed me through the temples.

"Look, Grandma—Magic Angel Unicorn is radiant with joy!"

"So I see." I pushed myself to my feet, pain doubling me over for a moment. Somewhere through the years, the bones and muscles holding me together had become molten lava. Or razor blades. I couldn't ever be sure whether I would go up in flames or be hacked to pieces from the inside out, but I was sure that eventually the pain would cast me into either insanity or complete despair.

My phone rang, and I picked it up, surprised to see Wynne's name instead of Al's. She seldom called, just sent texts full of emojis and the briefest of messages.

"Hi, Wynne." I took a few tentative steps away from the couch trying to loosen my legs. I'd need to go open the door when Al and the others came by for Andi.

"Mom?" Wynne's voice wavered, and I knew she wasn't calling with good news.

"What's wrong? Are you okay?"

"Mom, don't freak out. Mary called me." My legs shook as I walked into the kitchen, glad for once that Andrea was flying the unicorn around the living room ignoring me.

"They've been in a wreck, just coming into town. Al and Mary aren't badly hurt, but Caitlyn—" Wynne's voice shook. "Caitlyn's in surgery. My in-laws are keeping my boys. Steve and I are heading over in a few minutes. You shouldn't drive. Wait for us. We'll take you two to the hospital. We'll take turns staying with Andi in the waiting room."

"I'm here in town. I'll be fine—"

"No, Mom. Stay there. We don't want to make things worse. Just hang on. And pray."

The phone went dead, and I stared at it for a moment. Relief swamped me briefly—my firstborn was okay. Then the second part penetrated: his firstborn, my first grandchild, Caitlyn—. I couldn't finish the thought.

"Grandma, what's wrong?" Andrea came into the kitchen, still waving the stupid toy around. "Are you and Aunt Wynne mad? Mom always tells us Aunt Wynne is spoil—" she stopped. "Oops." She lowered her voice to a stage whisper. "Don't tell Grandma Aunt Wynne's spoiled, Magic Angel Unicorn."

"Andrea, sit down."

She did, but when she continued playing with the unicorn, kindness deserted me. So did patience.

I snatched the worn toy away and tossed it on the counter behind us.

She pouted and blinked back tears but didn't say anything.

I drew a deep breath and reached out to touch her cheek, feeling my hands tremble. "I didn't mean to lose my temper, but you need to listen. Your Aunt Wynne and Uncle Steve are coming—"

"Yay! The cousins! The cousins ride again!"

"Andi, your dad, mom and Caitlyn are at the hospital. They were in a wreck. We're going to go see them."

She looked at me blankly. "I don't get it," she said after a moment.

She didn't get—what? That her parents and sister were injured? That Caitlyn—again, I fought against the image. Not my granddaughter.

"It's just surprising," she said, so calmly that I suddenly feared she was in shock. "Because you know, Magic Angel Unicorn kissed all of them before they left. And Caitlyn took the little bag of magic unicorn fur I made for her."

A red haze formed between us, coming out of nowhere and falling like scarlet fog. I tried to struggle toward Andrea, but my intentions weren't clear, and it didn't matter. I dissolved into the red, then fell through that into darkness.

I woke to Wynne's hysteria and Steve's calm reassurances as he carried me down the steps toward their car.

"We should have called the ambulance," she told her husband with agitation. I felt sorry for him. Carrying me and trying to calm Wynne couldn't be easy.

"Andrea? Where's Andi—"

"Buckled into the car." They slid me into the seat next to her.

"Are you okay, Grandma?" Andi asked, then, not waiting for my answer, went on. "Wow. I wonder what the chances are that everyone in a family has to go to the hospital at the same time?"

Wynne turned and glared at both of us, although her eyes were swollen and red and tears had streaked her make-up. "Andrea, your Grandma fainted—or something. Your folks were in an accident. Maybe you should just talk about something else, okay?"

"Eh," Andi answered, and began making shapes with her hands.

"Why are you mad at me?" I muttered, and Wynne rubbed a hand across her face.

"My Pa's dead, my brother and niece are injured—and we walk in and think we lost you, too. I couldn't..." Her tone morphed from anger to unbearable hurt, and she turned away, ducking her head.

Beside me, Andrea started singing a unicorn song.

Football coaches in Texas work pretty much all summer, with conditioning, camps and then a contractual two-week head start on the rest of their colleagues. Once Caitlyn was out of ICU, and Al could quit crying every time he walked out of a visit with her, he went back to running the early football program. I took up a permanent post in her room. The beauty of being a retired teacher was that I could do that, sit for hours and just watch her sleep, or struggle to smile when someone came to poke or prod or take more blood from her uninjured arm,

"Grandma," Caitlyn said one morning, "you should go home." She smiled faintly. "The doctors said I might go home in three or four days."

The smile brightened. "And I'm lucky. It's not my writing and pitching arm that's hurt."

You're lucky to be alive.

"Why do you do that?" she asked, weariness and boredom creeping back into her voice.

"Do what?"

"Cross yourself when you pray." She shifted around in bed. Dad told me you're not Catholic and Aunt Rachel doesn't do that."

I shrugged. "Forty-three years with your grandpa and *tías*. It just feels right. Like something that makes a prayer—official, you know?"

"Oh." Her head moved against the pillow, but her eyes closed, then jerked open. "You should go home for a while, Grandma. I'll be fine. And asleep."

"I'll stay a little longer. Sweet dreams."

Her lips quirked slightly. "I'll prob'ly dream about Andi and her unicorns," she mumbled, and dozed off.

Hours later, the 'unicorn thing' bubbled over unexpectedly. One of the rotating doctors was in the room while Mary and Andrea visited. I'd gone home to shower and change and walked in again to find a full room. The doctor frowned over Caitlyn's chart and shook her head a little.

"I don't like this," she mused, more to herself than anyone. Mary was off near the corner, and Andi was standing next to the doctor as if she were a consultant, dirty unicorn in hand.

"What's wrong?" I asked, fearfully. "Doctor—"

"Hoffsteader," the woman replied. "I'm—"

Andrea cracked up. "Hoffsteader! What a funny name! We could change it to Hoofsteader, then it would be a unicorn name. Get it? Hoofsteader?"

The doctor glared. This hospital, like many, hired doctors who rotated in from San Antonio, were around for a few days, then left until their next turn. I guessed no one else had been rude enough—or childish enough—to ridicule this doctor's name.

"Perhaps someone could take this young lady to the waiting room?" Dr. Hoffsteader jerked her head in the direction of the door. Angry rather than embarrassed, Mary came out of her corner and hugged Andi's shoulders briefly.

"You stay," she told me. "I don't really understand much about all the stuff they keep claiming is wrong with poor Caitie."

Dr. Hoffsteader watched them go, then turned to me, raising an eyebrow. "Your granddaughters?"

"Yes, both." I glanced at Caitlyn. "Doctor—"

"The readings don't look great right now. There could be an infection. We're going to need to keep her a few more days and see if the white blood cells look better."

Behind her, Caitlyn moaned softly in protest. "I need to be home before school starts." She tried to smile, although her eyes glinted with tears. "I'm starting high school."

Dr. Hoffsteader nodded. "We'll do what we can." She turned back to me, holding the chart out to me, and beginning to explain in detail. I looked, and tried to listen, but kept hearing Andrea's shrieks of laughter cutting through Caitlyn's quiet despair. How on earth were those two even related?

"You're home for the Belmont Stakes," I told Caitlyn as she walked over to perch on the couch. She'd lost color and weight, but having her visit me so soon after her release from the hospital filled me with joy.

I blinked back tears, but she saw and grinned. "Of all the traits I could have inherited from you, I got the crying-all-the-time thing," she teased.

I shrugged. "Keep crying," I advised her. "It's what we do. Especially when we're this happy."

She eased her legs up, and I focused on her face, rather than her still bandaged right calf. "Remind me about the race," she ordered. "I've been sort of...gone."

"Yeah. Justify might win the Triple Crown this year. He got the Derby and Preakness."

"The Belmont's the long one, right?"

I nodded, pleased with her. My kids had been coming over to watch the Triple Crown races for most of their adult lives, and I didn't think they had a clue about which race was what.

"It's been around almost as long as the U.S.," I added.

"A horse won a couple of years ago, right? The Triple Crown."

"Yes. It's funny—you might see two Triple Crown winners before you're fourteen. I was eighteen before I saw one."

"Secretariat," she said, satisfied that she knew.

We were silent for a few minutes. I remembered the times she had called over several years to tell me that the Secretariat movie was on—or *The Sound of Music*. They had called Caitlin my mini-.me when she attended the school where I taught first grade. I couldn't imagine why.

My smile faded suddenly as I realized her sister hadn't come. "Is Andi okay, Caitlyn?"

She blushed and moved slightly, wincing. "Uh...she didn't want to come, Grandma. She's home with Mom."

I'm still in the doghouse, then. Apparently, Mary felt scolding Andrea was uncalled for after the unicorn-doctor fiasco. Even though I defended myself, explaining that someone should just let Andi know that making fun of names was rude and uncalled for....

The code pinged and the door lock whirred, and Al came in, looking tired. "A hundred and three already," he greeted us. "Half the team puked during drills."

He leaned over and kissed Caitlyn. "Your mom and sister are waiting outside," he told her. "You go ahead. I'm stealing water from your grandma."

Caitlyn managed to get up and limp off before we reached the kitchen.

"They should have come in and said hello," I told Al as he pulled water and a soda from the refrigerator.

"Really, Ma?" He raised an eyebrow at me and shook his head. "Andrea cried for two hours that day you went after her."

"Went after her?" I was outraged. "I explained that you don't make fun of a person's name. It's a conversation you and your mother should have had with her."

Al put the soda down and drained half the bottle of water. "Mary told me you were horrible to her."

Mary left you for six months after Caitlyn was born, I thought, but didn't remind him. Postpartum depression was real. I'd gotten through it myself. Without leaving Al or his father. But the problem was with Andi.

No. The problem was unicorns. Stupid damn unicorns.

"Al, be reasonable. The doctor trying to take care of Caitlyn—your daughter, too, you know—was furious. I almost died of embarrassment, and Caitlyn probably did, too. I didn't bring you up to insult strangers. All I did—"

"Was go off on how rude and childish she was. How there are no unicorns. God, Ma—half the girls in the world her age or younger are into unicorns."

"Fourth graders don't go to the grocery store wearing unicorn horns, Al. They don't laugh hysterically over a name that might not be common in south Texas but isn't uncommon. Fourth graders should know the difference between fantasy and reality—you know what? I taught that for 20 years in first grade. First grade!"

"She knows the difference," he muttered darkly.

"No! No, I don't think she does. And that could expose her to ridicule, and labeling—how can you want that for her? Have you ever thought that if you were out in public somewhere and were distracted—all anyone would have to do to lure her away would be to tell her she should go see the unicorn right around the corner?"

He swore under his breath and left the kitchen, stopping in the living room. "So, she likes unicorns. Her friends give her unicorn things. So do her mother and I. So do Wynne and the cousins. What the hell is wrong with that?" He paused, flinging the bottle away when he realized it was empty.

"Have you seen your Facebook feed, Ma? Every other post is a damn horse! You collected horses for years. How is that different?"

"Horses are real." His argument stunned me. Could he really not see—I shook my head jerkily. "Of all the asinine arguments. Al, I *had* horses. And ponies. Twenty-five of them. I boarded horses. I trained horses. Horses are *real*."

"Are they?" He, too, shook his head. "Are they real for you, Ma? Will you ever have one again? Or ride one again? You talk about visiting strangers who have horses to ride with them, and you can't walk down steps safely—." His voice broke off, and color flooded his face. For moments, I thought my unflappable son would cry. Instead, he walked over and hugged me.

"I'm so sorry," he murmured. "That was wrong. It's just—Andi gets crushed so easily. If you and she could be close—maybe cut her just a little slack. Ma?" He kissed my cheek. "I love you," he added, then gave me a slight smile. "Of course, knowing you, you might not believe that."

He stopped at the front door. "We'll come see you Saturday," he added. "Wynne, too. We're bringing food." He looked at the alcove in the hall. Soft light illuminated the urn with his father's ashes.

"This is the second year he won't be complaining over watching a horse race instead of *fútbol*." He closed the door softly, and I heard the gears in the lock whir, locking me in.

Saturday, June 9th, 2018. The house was full for the 150th running of the Belmont Stakes. Family filled me in a way that nothing else came close to doing. *Except horses.* The thought pierced the contentment wrapped around me. Lively and loud, all my grandkids, my two children, and their respective spouses covered all the seating in the living room.

From my end of the couch, I could see the dining table filled with food—fried chicken and fries, a cake—all the makings of a celebration the way the kids had always known them. Raul would have complained about watching the race, but he always mentioned the first Belmont Stakes we'd watched all those years ago. And whatever difficulties he and I encountered, his love for his children and grandchildren had always been rock solid. Real.

The call to the post still gave me goosebumps. Ten magnificent thoroughbreds walked onto the track.

"So does he win?" Al asked, and everyone looked at me.

Everyone but Andrea. I heard her in the hall somewhere, talking to her unicorn and who knew what other mythical figures.

The cameras were focused firmly on Justify, a huge chestnut. Big red—like Secretariat. But watching him, I felt detached. The excitement and magic weren't as strong, if I felt them at all. But all those eyes were watching me instead of the screen.

"This one's tough," I admitted. "He's undefeated. But he didn't win the Preakness with much to spare, and the Belmont's the longest of the race." I looked up at the ceiling as if the answer might be scrolled across the orange panels. "He's got a good trainer..."

"But will he win?" everyone chorused.

"Yeah. Sure." I said, seconds before the gate clanged open. But I didn't think he would.

Two minutes later, another big chestnut stood in the winner's circle, draped in white carnations. The thirteenth horse to claim the Triple Crown out of over a hundred who had tried.

Justify had been good enough after all.

But the magic just didn't come.

Andi clattered toward the kitchen, stopping right in front of the TV set, and glanced at me. "So, Grandma—who won?"

My kitchen and my home were suddenly full of magic. "A horse named Unicorn," I said.

***

Old Poems and Old Swifties

My love of music has been on hiatus—I lost my hearing on Valentine's Day of 2024. As I often did, I had music on while I wrote. The last song I heard then was Taylor Swift's "Mine."

Clearly, I'm behind the curve just a little on her music, because that was one of her very early songs. But I loved the first music she released, enough that I didn't play much else.

My youngest daughter and I came to verbal blows when Taylor released "Fifteen." The song mentions Tim McGraw, and she was offended (maybe because she adored Tim herself) that Taylor would "use him just to become better known." I told her that I thought Taylor was brilliant, and I wished I could think of some way to use his name to bring my writing to everyone's attention.

Of Taylor's early songs, my favorite was "Love Story."

Unable to sing, I wrote poetry during much of my early years. The second or third time I saw the video for "Love Story," it reminded me of one of the poems I wrote years earlier. I remember distinctly that I wrote it in a green notebook when I was working at a hardware store in the payment office. (I'm a conscientious person, I swear. But sometimes we didn't get a single payment all day. I had to do something.)

When I decided to put together *Always the Moon*, a book of my poetry, I threw away many of my handwritten poems—trying to break another Cancer habit—clinging. One of the items I threw away was that green spiral notebook. I'm glad that by then, I had included it in a book of my poetry.

Here's *Encounters*, my version of a love story:
"I've known you forever."
Yeah. Right. Tell it to the Marines.
"No, really. You were here before,
In a colonial gown.
We danced—

You wore gardenias then,
Not orchids.
Your hair was different, not dark.
But I knew you—
Have known you—
Always."
"And you're here again?
Asking me out?—
No. It's a clever lie,
But a lie. We just met."
"You like roses better even
Than gardenias, you don't like
An orchid's artificial feel—
I'm surprised that you wear one
Now.
"Well—"
"The roses have to be red though—
Blood red—
It has to do with our first meeting,
Eons ago
Back when time first began."
"Still—"
He laughed, brushed tears
From my cheeks, his touch
Familiar,
And intimate.
"You grow zinnias better than roses, though."
Who doesn't?
"Drink cocoa
With three marshmallows and cinnamon.
You stare at the moon until it explodes
Inside you,

Drives you almost
To madness.
Babies
Break your heart—
"Babies and the moon.
I was never
Your first passion."
"Yes. But then you know that I'm married,
Alone,
Embittered,
Afraid—"
"But not of me, even though
You should be—
You should fear us—
Above all, because we
Could be again
What we were once."
"*I won't hear this—*"
"No. You never would."
In his eyes, infinite sadness,
Clocks chiming midnight...
Seconds later, silence.
"No," he said again, the word flat
And without anger.
"You're right. There was only then,
Only once
When I knew you—goodbye."
He smiled, a polite social smile
And was gone.
I saw him again,
Later on,
Years later,

Dancing with someone.
I turned to go,
Hoping
He knew me still.

Hating someone in the spotlight has become the norm over the years, which is sad. If we could all write music, or play a sport at a professional level, or discover a cure for cancer, why should those abilities be condemned instead of admired?

Taylor is where she is because of her talent and drive. And despite the fame, with the adulation and the dangers that come with fame now, she doesn't strike me as bitter or particularly demanding.

I have three brothers and a sister in Florida—in the area devastated by Milton. Taylor gave millions to both Helene and Milton victims. How can anyone not appreciate that, especially if they themselves are not able to help?

At one time, I watched more baseball than football. But both my sons and three of my grandsons either played or now play football, so I have become a football fan. And if I see someone cheering for a loved one—I'm fine with that.

A romance author whose work I know—who started writing when I did, but is much more successful—is writing a football romance. And yes, it was inspired by Taylor and Travis.

I couldn't be happier for her— or them.

I can't hop planes and score tickets to show that at heart I'm a Swiftie—but I don't mind admitting I think she's a fabulous entertainer and a terrific person.

When I can hear again, I have some serious catching up to do on music—beginning with Taylor's.

***

A Writer's Nightmare

A knife wound to the heart couldn't have wounded more profoundly. An hour earlier, I had put aside my manuscript to double check the spelling of a name used in the story. The story was finished. I'd written "The End." And it was due in my editor's office at the end of the day—in half an hour, in other words.

I'd turned off my computer on the theory that my computer wouldn't hassle me the way it did if I treated it with more compassion. I should turn it off when I didn't need it. So, I had turned it off.

That was the kind, "be a better person" me.

Then I turned on my well-rested desktop to send the manuscript and impress all the higher ups with my professionalism.

Only—the computer didn't work right when I turned it back on.

The better person me morphed into my more common self—frustrated me.

The frustrated me unleashed a string of words in two languages that no one should have to hear. Still the screen blinked "File Corrupted."

The computer genie helpfully asked if I was sure I wanted those words recorded.

The somewhat tech-savvy person took all the right steps—trying to recover, rebooting, praying, checking to see if the manuscript was saved somewhere in space.

File Corrupted. File Corrupted.

File Corrupted? I snorted. That stupid program would see corrupted.

I checked the little tray of medicines next to the laptop. I'd taken the diabetes meds. Blood pressure pill, check.

Calmly I stood up, picked up the printer, which had never worked well, and smashed the printer into the laptop, throwing a few more profanities at the pile of junk.

Then I picked up a notebook and pen and headed for the breakroom for my secret chocolate stash before punching in my editor's phone number.

***

[Author's note: The perks of being a successful author are breathtaking: traveling, meeting royalty, winning awards...and then, there are the moments that the yet-to-achieve successful author status lives.]

Time Penalties

I look ridiculous pacing around a tiny front stoop in an evening gown. To make matters worse, I have to hold the skirt off the tiles, because I'm sharing the small space with obnoxious, smelly pigeons who want me gone. I can't glance at my watch to see the time because it's covered by the pristine white gloves I thought the occasion demanded. But a beep from under the gauzy fabric tells me that it's six o'clock.

She's going to be late. Heck, they're going to be late! Didn't I raise a single one of four kids right? Respect others. Be on time. Expect unforeseen delays. Be on time anyway. I remembered chanting that advice, using it like a mantra, or a litany.

Apparently, not one of the four learned a thing.

At half past, they pull up in my oldest son's truck. It's shiny, new, and white, but the resemblance to fairy tale horses ends there. Climbing up into that thing will take me another half hour—if I can do it at all in a ballgown.

"You're late," I mutter, as my elder daughter Jamie and second son Greg help me down the stairs, while the oldest holds the door and my youngest daughter crumples the skirt of my gown into a ball and trails after us.

"We're late!" I'm so mad, I'm shaking. Could be the exertion of getting into the truck, but I feel sick to my stomach. That is what happens whenever I'm late. In my adult life, I have been late once. By a minute. And the store owner—my boss—deliberately reprimanded me, saying I was always on time just to show others up.

"You shouldn't stress, Mom," Jamie scolds. "Not good for you. Besides, we'll only be a little late. You said yourself this award you're nominated for isn't important."

"One award ceremony! One! And you can't pick me up on time? Why?"

The oldest, Chuy, takes his eyes off the road and looks into the rearview mirror. He smiles, the way he always does and melts my heart. "I had to gas up, Mom," he offers.

"And I guess you needed to stop at Walmart, Jamie?"

"No, not this time. I swear. And I was almost ready when Chuy came. We should have been here in plenty of time."

"So, you were asleep, Greg?"

"I woke up the second time they honked. No biggie."

"No biggie? I'm nominated for Breakout Writer of the Year, the first annual Amazon World award, and it's no big deal? First prize is $50,000 and a date with real English royalty as inspiration!"

My watch beeps again. We are really, really late. The pickup, new as it is, looks ridiculous inching along between Rolls and limos. When we finally reach the carpeted aisle leading in, a doorman helps me out. "We'll park and come in," they all chime in unison. "Good luck."

An hour and a half later, I smiled as I received a small trophy and certificate. So, fifth wasn't quite the same as a fortune and a prince, but something was something.

The lady at my table congratulated me when I sat down again. "Sorry your kids didn't get here," she commiserated, then lowered her voice. "You know, though, something weird happened. When they announced the nominees, they announced your name first. You weren't here yet. But they looked all over, and then they sort of shuffled envelopes. I noticed that when they gave out the awards—it was in the order they'd announced them at the beginning—except for yours."

She shrugged and patted my arm. "Don't think a thing of it, though. Surely there aren't any late penalties in writing."

"Surely," I assured her through gritted teeth and stood. "Excuse me. I need to call a cab."

"No, look, dear—there come your children. Just in time."

***

Cadillac Cat

Now I know why they're called "pick 'em up" trucks—but have cats no conscience at all?

Once a year, like a bath, whether you need it or not—even after 15 years of good professional evaluations, knowing an administrator is dropping into my first-grade classroom makes me anxious. Walk-ins, visitors I don't mind, but make it "the" formal assessment of my teaching abilities, and I go so far as to dust computers and clean my desk.

Knowing that I would need extra caffeine to get through the day, I ran over to the local convenience store on my way to work this morning. The store isn't the closest, but the clerks are faster and minimally more courteous, so I generally drive the extra few blocks.

As I got out of my pickup, the official vehicle of Texas—I noticed an orange cat near the front bumper, mewing plaintively. It looked like one of my daughter's adopted strays, and I muttered a silent curse at people who abandon cats in public places with busy parking lots. The cat would be sure to meet a tragic end, but we had enough cats, and anyway, I had to get to work early and dust my desk.

Again.

I pushed aside the nagging thoughts about the poor, abandoned cat and went to get my can of diet caffeine.

If one needs to be somewhere early, one should know that an emergency will arise and make one late.

Most of Laredo's 300,000 residents had stopped for tacos that morning, and the one clerk at that store who genuinely hates me was there, cell phone trapped between his chin and ear as he tried to attend customers.

By the time I got out, I'd forgotten all about the poor cat.

Until it mewed at me as I walked toward the truck, and then stood on its hind legs to sniff the grill.

That's when it hit me: I was the wretch who'd abandoned a cat by the city's busiest street.

The cat was my daughter's latest project, a stray she wanted to tame enough to take to the vet. She would, she promised, then find it a good home.

She really believes that's possible, even in a city with too many stray animals roaming the streets.

The cat—Sunny? —did have a fondness for sleeping on the hood, but I hadn't seen her there that morning, and I had checked under the truck, as I always do. Either she'd ridden the eight or ten blocks on the roof of the cab or in the bed. Or, worse—somewhere in the engine compartment.

My momentary relief over her safety gave me an immediate headache—what the heck was I supposed to do now?

The evil me said she was too wild to catch, she'd never let me put her in the truck, and maybe she'd find a good home if she stayed.

The real me started cooing and easing toward her—and darned if she didn't just let me pick her up.

Okay, but she'd claw me on those few short steps to the truck, jump out of the bed—and if I put her inside, she'd poop out of stress and fear.

Telling myself I could eventually clean up whatever she did to the truck, and I couldn't leave her, I opened the door, pushed her in—and was amazed when she made no last-ditch effort to claw my eyes out and escape.

By the time I pulled up alongside our picket fence and climbed out, the cat and I were good buddies. She looked at me serenely as I held the door like a private chauffeur, sniffed a little, and jumped out. A minute later, she'd squirted through the wrought iron bars, and I was off to dust my desk. Covered in cat hairs.

Oh, well.

Righteousness over appearance. Guess Sunny will have to go under the section about cats and Murphy's Law.

***

And Their Cowboys

My childhood days were dotted with heroes—western heroes, named Trigger, Buttermilk, Silver, *Diablo* and Tornado. Fast and fearless, my four-legged loves galloped over rough, arid badlands or through lush valley grasses, confronting evil and saving the world on a weekly basis. In those early days, I really didn't notice much about television except horses—and as an aside, the cowboys that rode them. But the horses were the thing.

Life being what it is, there came a time when the men on those horses started catching my eye, too. The cowboy as hero—stoic, honest, able to love just one woman for a lifetime, thinking of his horse before himself, courageous, handsome—forced itself into my consciousness. I wrote a John Wayne script during high school chemistry class—because John Wayne would doubtlessly have a young, good looking cowboy sidekick riding with him. Unfortunately, John Wayne never got to shoot that movie—the script was burned when my father disowned me for marrying a dude ranch cowboy. But the palomino the sidekick would have ridden in the movie—Taj—would have been golden. Pun intended.

Kids move on. I traded western stock horses for Arabians and Thoroughbreds—-the hot bloods of the equine world. I rode in an English saddle and decided that the idea of stoic, honest, faithful men was fiction at best, and likely just an evil lie perpetuated over time. With the onslaught of social media, though, I kept up with the original horses I'd cherished as a kid—the paints and quarterhorses, the Appaloosas that had been my favorites for a brief time when I saw the Disney movie about them. I picked Derby winners and dreamed of show jumpers, but I never got away from those good, solid steeds that used to save the world on Saturdays.

And their cowboys. The cowboys came over time to hold a larger part in my fantasies than their horses. Looking back, I realize I was either getting old or growing up—but the men with their honesty, fairness, good looks and occasional bare chests had become the heroes. They were the ones defeating evil, loving one woman for a lifetime, suffering unbearable pain and still moving forward with courage and kindness. I found myself loving cowboys more than their horses.

Well, maybe just as much.

Writing about women who love cowboys comes naturally and from the heart—I've been doing it since eleventh grade chemistry. With the wisdom of years spent living at a distance from that life, though, I can see flaws in both cowboys and their horses—but I know that I, and countless others, became who we are because of that love for a special kind of man, the cowboy. Even if the cowboy is an illusion, it's the kind of illusion that inspires and fills hearts.

If you're lucky enough to have your own real-life cowboy—wow!

Maybe you have a horse *and* its cowboy. Don't even buy a lottery ticket—you've hit the jackpot.

As Roy and Dale would croon, "Happy Trails to you..."

***

And Our Horses Came In—uh, Cowboys

I mentioned way back at the beginning that in 2013, I received my first acceptance from Crimson Romance for a romance set in south Texas. *Unattainable* is still my favorite of the CR books, which are still available through Simon & Schuster. And in 2013, lightning struck twice. D'Ann Lindun, also a CR author, and I became friends. Out of the blue late one night (or maybe it was earlier in Colorado, but I'm always up so it was perfect) she reached out to me about participating in *Cowboy Up*. The idea worried me a little—the deadline didn't seem far enough way, I was still teaching, and I'd never really focused on cowboys—I mean, the horses were my heroes.

Thankfully, I listened to D'Ann, who introduced me to other participating authors, who I still consider friends. Chief among them because of the central part she played is Melissa Keir, who was the ramrod, the financial genius, a brilliant writer, and a patient soul who still helps me stay sane.

The result of the collaboration went viral—we reached number 1 in virtually every country in the world on October 7th of 2014. Meanwhile, *Unattainable* was chugging up the list at Amazon, and reached either 3 or 5—I don't remember where that photo is saved. But that was honestly the only day out of 22 years when I had my phone next to me, open to Amazon, and checked it compulsively.

The takeaway for writers? Maybe embrace the human characters a little more than the horses—especially if the characters are cowboys.

***

Skinny Dipping Fully Clothed

Cold water seeped through the thick denim, chilling my legs, and making it hard to push forward. March wasn't the best time of the year to plunge into Lake Casa Blanca fully clothed. The man-made lake was shallow, and usually warm, but the deluge of rain two days had filled the lake to its capacity and reduced the temperature from its normal boiling point.

The inaccuracy amused me, and no one was around to question specifics. Even on the Texas-Mexico border, lakes didn't boil.

Why? Water boils at 112°.

The cloudy water rose higher, soaking my tee shirt.

Wait! 212! Of course, lakes don't boil, even in Laredo. Some summer they might, though.

The buoyancy kicked in, and my feet wanted to leave the bottom of the lake. That wouldn't help. Far off, a motorboat pulled anchor and sputtered my way, annoying me.

It sped past, its occupants waving and smiling at me.

I waved back, not smiling, feeling the small wake from the boat rock me, and water tickle my chin.

My feet came up off the bottom, and I floundered forward, swimming a few strokes automatically. Almost nothing my mother told me had ever been true, but this one thing had—you don't forget how to swim.

Behind me, sudden noise interrupted the peaceful absence of life around me.

Since I didn't think I would have the resolve to plant my feet on the bottom and stay there long enough to drown myself, I swam a few yards toward the shore and checked out the shoreline.

School buses! Damn it to bloody hell! Students were spilling out the narrow doors, many still wearing masks, all carrying the prerequisite bags of goodies to get them through the morning.

Automatically I glanced at the bus. Great. Catholic school buses. In the Catholic church, killing oneself is a sin. Plus, I had met several teachers from the school recently when I went to verify some information in a magazine our press was working on.

Maybe I could tiptoe by and to my car, now lost among a herd of yellow rocks. Mixed metaphors, yeah. Just the way I rolled. And wrote if I hung onto my job much longer.

There was a mad stampede as kids—second or third graders, I guessed—scrambled for their choices of tables and awnings. Some skipped the practical part and rushed the swings and see-saws.

A couple of little girls gaped at me.

One waved shyly. When I waved back, water from my sopping sleeve ran from my wrist back to my elbow, defying the natural science of anatomy.

And suddenly, there she was—head teacher of the Catholic academy, Sister Mary Antonia Gallegos.

She gaped, too, her eyes widening and her mouth opening, and walked toward me with purpose.

I left the Catholic Church at seventeen, and I was still afraid of nuns and their rules.

"Sister," I greeted her, nodding. "How are you?"

She didn't answer, just looked me up and down.

"Were you trying to drown yourself?" she asked sternly, ignoring my greeting.

Never lie to priests and nuns. My mom preached that to me growing up. I attended Catholic grade school and had been reasonably convinced that I would burst into flames and disintegrate if I lied to any member of the cloth.

Mom moved on from the Church when I was eleven and she divorced my father. I relished the structure and hope faith gave me then, but around seventeen, sinning seemed worth risking blowing myself up in flames.

But now, Sister was still looking at me, waiting. "No," I assured her, forcing a smile. "Just decided to go skinny dipping fully clothed."

"Skinny dipping?" she asked, raising her eyebrows.

No reason a nun should know the joys of plunging into water naked, right?

"You know, swimming uh, you know. Without clothes" I explained. "But since it's a public place, I thought I should wear all my clothes—"

"But you didn't, Ms. Roberts." She shook her head, her frown deepening. "Next time you decide to drown yourself, please wear a bra."

She clucked her disapproval and walked off. I saw her arm move slightly, and knew she was crossing herself after praying for me.

I lost myself among the clutter of buses, thinking. Schools often—usually, mostly—took their end-of-year field trips on Thursdays, to escape the extended day and tutorials, or on Friday—because Friday.

If I still felt like "skinny dipping with my clothes on," I could come back next Monday.

Satisfied with myself, I climbed into my little car and headed home.

Walking into the office on Monday didn't feel a lot different than wading into the tepid waters of Lake Casa Blanca. My shoes dragged through the thick carpet as if stuck in bottom mud.

Wendy Stone glanced away from her computer screen and nodded at me. "Hey, Rosie," she whispered, but immediately refocused on her screen.

Her reaction warned me before the squeak of the door that Sandy Guevara, the HR manager, had come into the room.

I went straight to my corner desk by the window—one of few benefits of having been the original employee at Border Press and Prose.

When I started, eighteen years ago and new to Laredo with its border culture and the river that once bound two countries—a hopelessly romantic idea to the young woman I had been—my boss

Molly had been a chain-smoking woman in her late fifties who liked to define herself as "a passionate old broad with a plan."

Molly's brash persona and uncanny gift for trends and hits made her a star in a tough business to crack. She started printing chapbooks and providing miscellaneous services for Laredo's influx of businesses, and left others in the dust when it came to acquiring new technology.

BPaP, as Molly dubbed her little press, grew into a legend completely in keeping with the legendary status of Laredo, the Rio Grande, and Mexico, just across the river.

I grew up, really, alongside my boss. I quit partying, mostly, and took writing and editing seriously, no matter how insignificant the projects were. As BpaP grew and Molly became a legend herself, my skills grew along with my exposure to a whole world of characters, from local celebrities to deadbeats, politicians to bag ladies. I thought of Sister Mary Antonia. For some reason, the new, agnostic me usually caught the assignments to do PR for churches or their schools, for clergy moving into Laredo or leaving.

I didn't regret a minute of the time I worked with Molly, and then the others who came in as we grew.

Until the Change. A year and a half ago, Molly asked me to go out for drinks, something we seldom did any longer. We sat at a corner table but were constantly surrounded by her friends and admirers.

Even a couple of critics dropped by, berating her for the column in her newest venture, the online magazine *Get Real*.

"They're right, you know," she whispered, before they were completely out of earshot. "You can't fix stupid, now can you?"

I laughed and nodded agreement and reached for my drink.

She reached out and covered my hand with hers, and my heart stopped. Whatever she was about to tell me, I knew I didn't want to hear it.

Then she told me that she no longer owned Border Press and Print—an outside conglomerate with corporate offices in California thought the time was right to buy her out. And she had cancer and maybe two months to live.

"Depending," she added with her little laugh that still had a hint of her Irish ancestry, "on His Holy hand in the matter."

She died three weeks later.

I died right then and there.

But here I was, eighteen months after faceless, profit-driven big businesspeople had taken over, walking, talking, writing like a robot.

And apparently, I had pissed Human Resources off again. Ms. Guevara marched over to my desk and slapped an envelope on the corner.

"What is this?" I asked, rubbing my arms as goosebumps warned me that it wasn't a raise or commendation for an article of mine that had been picked up by a lifestyle journal.

"Your severance pay." She stood by my desk with her arms folded, and even Sister Mary Antonio had regarded me with more softness. "If you accept your termination, we will recommend you if someone expresses interest in you."

"But why?"

Wendy's sudden scrape of her chair and gasp startled me, and when I glanced at her, her face told me a lot. Whatever the reason I was being fired, she probably had unwittingly had a hand.

"We had very extensive training on what we expect from our employees when we bought out this little concern." Ms. Guevara shifted on her feet but didn't uncross her arms or make a single facial gesture. "You were warned then—and recently—that we do not permit offensive, past century attitudes and views. We're a progressive concern, Ms. Roberts. Your former boss held BpaP back with her archaic views and publishing choices."

"What the hell are you talking about?" Being blunt couldn't hurt, I supposed, if I was already fired.

"We specifically said there would be no posturing on abortion here. You are not a doctor or a clergy member, and you were arguing against the pro-choice movement. We print hundreds of jobs for them."

"I told her that I asked you for your advice," Wendy told me miserably from across the room. "I needed someone I trusted to—"

"Ms. Stone, you're on the edge here, too. Finish your work and mind your own business. Remember that you're an at-will employee just like she was."

I stood up, glad I was a little taller than Ms. Guevara. My height had been a handicap when I tried to drown myself but being able to look down on this contemptible woman literally and figuratively gave me pleasure.

"So, because I'm anti-abortion—anti killing babies for non-medical reasons—I can no longer write?"

"You signed consent forms when you stayed on with us. Your social media is full of unacceptable posts."

"Because I condemned rioting and looting? Because I said I won't vote for anyone in the next election if none of the candidates meet my expectations?"

"We vote in this office," Ms. Guevara retorted, then turned away, stopping to look back at me. "If you want to fight it, do. But we have you dead to rights."

She slammed the door as she left.

Wendy was in tears. "I don't know why I asked—"

I smiled at her. "For a friend, you said. Whatever your friend decides—and it is her choice—this isn't your fault, girl."

"Girl?" she parroted, and we both laughed through teary eyes—we weren't supposed to use gender-specific names for each other, either. Just last names if we had customers in the room or given names if not.

Fifteen minutes later, the last twenty years of my life were fading in my rear-view mirror.

Monday was scorching hot, and nobody was at the lake. I'd been right in my assumption there wouldn't be school buses today.

I sat under an awning finishing my chicken for one, revisiting odds and ends from my life. Usually, one resorted to suicide out of depression, or some life-changing event. I wasn't depressed—angry maybe, and a little sad, but not depressed. Just...annoyed. Annoyed beyond reason, and too unbending to look for reasons to go on.

Besides, I reminded myself, I could change my mind any time. It's not like Lake Casa Blanca had eighty-foot depths or raging currents.

And I was just skinny-dipping fully clothed.

I had been skinny dipping the night I decided to leave the church. The water in a north Georgia stream was much colder than the water in a shallow south Texas lake. A lot of it was just disappointment—in myself, in a world I no longer understood.

In life.

I cleaned up my area carefully and threw the trash away. A hamburger wrapper, driven by rising wind, fluttered against my foot. I picked it up and threw it too, knowing that all the little disappointments—like being responsible again, when others weren't always—was one of those little annoyances I had come to resent in the last year and a half.

"Windy day," a man said behind me, and I jumped and turned around.

He works out. A lot. And he's really young.

I stared. Then I remembered something Molly used to say. "Girlfriend, look all you want. But don't drool. Just keep your tongue in your mouth and don't drool."

A sob—or laughter? —caught in my throat. I turned and walked toward the water.

Maybe he'd think I'd take everything off if I went in, get grossed out, and leave...

At the water's edge, I paused. I didn't have to look around to know that he had followed me but wasn't standing close enough to scare me.

"You're Daphne Roberts, right?" When I didn't answer and took a few steps toward the water, he stepped in front of me and held out his hand.

"Guy Madrigal," he announced, catching my hand even though I didn't move it away from my leg. "You know my aunt. She thought I might find you here."

"I don't know any Madrigals, and you're stalking me, then."

"My aunt is Sister Mary Antonia, and my mother is her sister Patty."

He had dimples when he smiled, and I loved dimples. But he was maybe twenty-one and related to the only authority figure I still feared.

"Why would she send her nephew to harass me?" *If he calls me "Karen" I'll drown him, too.*

"She has a job for you. She saw a piece you wrote about the Alamo several months ago. Apparently, you felt the same way about it that she did."

I blinked. "Sister Mary Antonia wants me to write about the Alamo?"

"No. The cathedral. It's been here—how long?"

"Forever," I said succinctly, exaggerating a little. If I remembered, the current cathedral had been there since 1872 and replaced an earlier church. I shrugged. "I don't really write pieces about churches."

"Talk to her," he repeated. "I'll tell her you'll be in touch?"

I looked out over the motionless lake. An egret, startling in its whiteness, sailed onto land in shallow water nearby.

"The lake will be here tomorrow or in ten years," Guy said softly. "Come kill yourself later, if you have to."

I tried not to, but he was just so cute. And young, and unburdened. I smiled at him. "Tell your aunt I will call her later this afternoon to set up an appointment."

Two days later, I walked into the cathedral. My plan had been to sit in a back pew and soak in the ambience, but I found myself walking down the center aisle, drawn to the altar, then somehow, to the confessional.

I closed the door silently behind me. "Bless me Father for I have sinned," I said.

Eight days later, the lake was almost unrecognizable. A weekend of pummeling rain had hit the dry south Texas region causing flooding. Steady winds were beating an overflowing lake into a fair impression of Lake Michigan. Not that I'd ever seen Lake Michigan, but this sure wasn't Lake Casa Blanca.

I shivered, standing with cold water lapping at the toes of my sneakers. There were currents today, but no water birds flew by. There were wind warnings out to boaters, too, a completely different body of water than the one I had waded into just days ago.

I looked around, but Guy was nowhere to be seen. *Good,* I thought, but didn't really mean it. He'd been like an occasional shadow while I worked on the piece about San Augustin Cathedral, suddenly appearing like a blessing—or a curse—to distract me.

The problem with skinny dipping, I thought idly, is that people think they see you, standing there naked. But they don't, because—we all keep our clothes on, really.

With clothes on, it's easier to hide—from others, from God—from yourself.

Cold water seeped through the thick denim, chilling my legs, and making it hard to push forward. Waves battered me, pushing me back a step for every two I took forward. I moved robotically, stumbling when my feet wouldn't lift enough to avoid obstacles on the lakebed.

Water slapped my chin, hard, and I clamped my lips shut tightly to keep it out. Another foot or two, and the water should be over my head.

The wind gusted hard, bringing an ocean-worthy wave toward me. My feet came out from under me, and I let myself fall forward.

Then I swam.

***

That Thing About Lions

Ebenezer came home in the back compartment of the family station wagon. My sister Stephanie—Steve—and I were at the "development," checking on the Coke and Pepsi machines and dragging our feet about going inside. School was out for the summer, and to say that we had a regular schedule governing any part of our lives would be a stretch.

My sister and I turned at the crunch of tires on the graveled red clay drive. The gravel had been put down recently— red clay turns to red goo in rain. Cars get stuck in red goo.

"Looks like they brought someone home," Steve told me. "It's almost ten at night. Why—no, it's not a person."

By then, I quit ignoring her and squinted toward the drive, too. "Is that another Great Dane?" Mom and Dad raised Great Danes, and the animal in the back had that light golden color called fawn in dogs and blonde in women. Men, too, I guess. "If so, that's horrible—its neck is too fat. It doesn't—"

I stopped cold and stared harder. "What's a lion doing in the back seat?" I shrieked. I ran in the general direction of the car and the house and the lion, but Steve flew past me as if I were standing still.

The car door opened, and Mom got out first. She was a petite woman who favored pearls and navy for her job at the *Atlanta Journal* library. Tonight, though, when she turned around, the navy-blue dress had two huge paw prints on the back, as if some giant animal had clutched her close to whisper "You'll be dinner sometime, okay?"

"Mom—" Steve and I started in unison. "What—"

She forced a smile. "This is how you know you love someone, girls," she muttered. "When you're willing to let a lion hug you to prove that the lion your husband wants to buy is really tame." She looked back at the car and shuddered slightly. "Scariest moment of my life, when he stood on his hind legs, towering over me, and squeezed." Then she headed for the house where our other five siblings waited—blissfully

66

unaware that we were the proud but deranged owners of a lion named Ebenezer.

For the next few days and nights, the antebellum we lived in, with the rotted out corner and holes upstairs that allowed bats to fly in and out as if we were at the best-known bat watching site in Georgia, boasted a lion chained to a magnolia tree in the front yard. Walking out on the balcony and seeing Eb lying there, looking around regally, gave me a thrill. Made me feel all Ernest Hemingway-ish. Hadn't he written about lions? And he was well known. That feeling took me towards my destiny—writing best sellers that would be taught in English classes all over the world. Or maybe at least get me in *People Magazine*.

Our horses didn't read Hemingway. When I called them in to feed them, using the name order in which we had purchased them— "Smokey, Ali, Canter, Pom Pom—" what I would give *now* for a video tape of *then*. Twenty-six horses and ponies galloped from the pasture, into the yard—glanced at Ebenezer, tugging on his chain—and galloped away faster than they had come.

They didn't come back until Eb was up at the roadside amusement park site, which, still in its infancy, was just red clay with a shed and Coke and Pepsi machines.

The horses were my babies, so I'm a little embarrassed at how hard I laughed at the spectacle. You could almost hear Smokey and Ali, our first pony and horse respectively, say in that down south-Georgia drawl, "Lord have MERCY! I done run up on a lion."

That was the thing about having a lion. No one else did—we were special. Or thought so back then, when the rightful condemnation of keeping lions chained in front yards had not yet flourished.

There are, of course, many things about lions. Eb might have been a big overgrown pussycat—one who ate ten or fifteen pounds of chicken a day—but he *was* a cat. He hunted mice. And three-year-old brothers.

Just before Eb moved to a cage, my youngest brother, Chris, went out into the front yard. The Great Danes were with him—they went everywhere with him—and he was all curls, smiles, and a false sense of safety. He—as nearly as any of us knows, no one saw the episode—must have decided to pet the pretty kitty.

Those of us in the house heard the frenzied barks of two usually pacifist dogs who would ride off with a thief rather than defend the house. We rushed out to find Chris trapped under one of Eb's huge paws. His little arms and legs were flailing, as if he were trying to swim away from the lion. And whether Eb had selfish intentions, like a breakfast that wasn't chicken necks—the dogs had ticked him off, and he wasn't giving up his prize—my baby brother.

Somehow, we got the Danes, who were just protecting a family member, to realize they weren't helping and leave the scene. I left with them—I'm not good in lion-eating-family situations. I admit I just hid and cried, sort of a mantra of mine. (Although I'm not sure if back in those days, "mantras" were things.)

Long story short—Chris was okay except for some bruises. And Eb's cage was finished a couple of hours later.

Not that the cage was the kind of palatial enclosure you find in zoos these days. There was a small den, made from unpainted plywood anchoring a high wooden wall on one side. The other two sides were heavy gauge wire mesh. At least, it looked heavy on that first day. A narrow gate fastened with a padlock connected with the final wire mesh side, which ran back to the plywood hut. I suppose the whole cage was eight feet long by six—maybe. The point is, for a four-hundred-pound lion, the quarters were barely livable.

But Eb went in, the padlock went on—and my older sister and I celebrated. She saw a dude magnet, although I wasn't immediately aware of that. I saw a 4-H project that might be more competitive than the bug collections I usually took to the state competition. Or—a Hemingwayesque story.

My brother Greg inherited the abrupt title "zookeeper." Greg was the kindest, most loving guy in the world, but he had what horse people call "heavy hands." When he pet an animal, especially one of the family cats, it would flinch away. No matter how hard he tried to be gentle, the cats and dogs avoided him. With the arrival of an animal that outweighed him by more than three hundred pounds—and loved roughhousing—Greg found his kindred soul.

He fed Eb twice a day, cleaned the cage, wrestled with him—and not once did Eb pull away. Neither did Greg, although both Stephanie and I wound up with bites from a lion that was just that—a lion. That she only received a scar on her stomach and I on my knee might have been miraculous, looking back.

Starting an amusement park over fifty miles from Atlanta and outside a town of fewer than three hundred people wasn't brilliant, but to be honest—I loved the idea anyway. I figured at the time I would happily die there, surrounded by my horses and ponies, the snakes, the monkeys, the lion, and the peacocks.

Well, cancel the peacocks. As beautiful as they are, they're stupid, proud birds who stroll around demanding to be admired. Unfortunately, the birds—which cost over a hundred dollars each—had death wishes. The four pair we bought, plus their almost grown chicks, devised a game called "Show off for the lion."

One by one, they went into the cage. None of them came out. Another thing about lions is that they really don't mind eating around feathers—birds are prey, and even lions on chains in cages aren't safe to be around if you're a three-year-old or a peacock.

My sister's friends came to visit the lion—I mean her—a couple of times. By then we had an antique Ferris wheel, an airplane ride, and a merry-go-round. My dream was becoming sustainable. Both Steve and I tried to ignore the writing on the wall—on one visit, Eb reached out from under his cage wall and caught her friend Ed's shoes, pulling them off and coming close to dragging a foot in. Stephanie went in to save the shoes, Eb objected and grabbed her in the stomach, and Ed had to play the hero and help Stephanie escape. I don't remember exactly how he did that, but I do know—he never dropped by again. Which meant that I never saw his friend John again, and I didn't know anyone else in Meriweather County, Georgia, so I pretty much had decided I was in love with John.

Sadly—or happily, depending—my father was transferred back to Texas from Georgia. The horses and ponies were sold, then the monkeys, the snakes were turned loose, the jaguarundi and raccoons would move with us—and I watched Greg load Eb and the horrible macaque, a miniature chimp named Frankie, into cages on an old pickup truck taking them off to Savannah to attract attention at some gambling place.

The thing about lions is that when you have one, and lose it, you're really never free from the experience. Long into my working years, no longer a teenager, no longer in Georgia, I dreamed that Eb was starving. I needed to feed him, but I was afraid to do that. Eventually, in my dreams, I would go, knowing when I trekked up to the old mesh cage that Ebenezer would be dead, because I hadn't fed him in years. The guilt I felt, even knowing the truth when I woke up, that he was in Savannah, hopefully well cared for and surrounded by admirers, never eased: we should never have had a lion.

I haven't become Hemingwayesque, can't even say any longer that "I was dreaming of lions" after twenty or thirty years. But I don't beat myself up over having had Eb for that short time when I was a kid who felt more at home with critters than folks—I loved him.

There's one other thing about lions, if you've known one on a personal level. They're amazing animals.

They just don't belong in roadside exhibits run by kids to attract kids.

***

LEARNING TO WEAR RED

The pavement throbbed as I reached the door and music, laughter and alcohol fumes seeped into the hot darkness of a south Texas night. Going in was harder than I expected, but the arrival of a group of twenty-somethings pushed me forward and through.

Music, too loud and metallic, heightened my anxiety, and sweat beaded my forehead.

"*Mamacita*," someone murmured, pushing past. The crude flattery startled me, but the sexy young thing in the micro mini wrapping herself around the stranger in front of me made it clear the endearment hadn't been meant for me.

I was still just me, stodgy, unmoving and alone. Wondering why I had come.

Across the crowded room, Rosemary Molina suddenly stood up. Even from this distance, she was as intimidating as ever. Six feet or a shade taller, and...the old-world word would be 'voluptuous'. But the whole point of this agonizing night was to be younger and hipper, not trotting out words no longer popular because they weren't useful for texting. Hot. My grandkids would probably say she was hot.

"Aggie! Get over here, honky friend."

Heads turned my way, then her way, and there were giggles and stares.

When I was pregnant with my first child, I'd been grocery shopping a day after my due date, blissfully unaware of everything. My water broke, and filled with embarrassment, I thought I had wet myself. But there was no food at home, and seldom-there husband couldn't be counted on. So, I'd lifted my head and marched through the store like a robot, not giving in to embarrassment or fear.

Just as I did now.

Rosemary jiggled a little as she did some kind of stationary bounce, waiting for me to walk into her open arms and crushing me in an affectionate hug.

I patted her back uncomfortably and inched back. "Hi," I mumbled.

She laughed and waved at the bench opposite her. "Sit your ass down, girl. Can't believe you remembered me!" She plopped down and waved a hand toward a nearby waitress. "Well, that's not true. Who could forget me? Even after thirty years."

The waitress came over, and Rosemary motioned. "Bring my friend a—" She arched a thin eyebrow at me. "What, Honky?"

"Diet Coke?"

Rosemary shook it off. "That's not a bar drink. Are you driving home?"

"No, but—"

"Then try a strawberry daiquiri. That's enough of a sissy drink anyway."

Rosemary ordered straight whisky for herself, and laughed when someone passing by leaned over and whispered into her ear.

"Don't worry. He wasn't talking about you," she assured me. "Although, you know—he'd come sit with us if you want."

"Why would I want that?" Contempt crept into my voice. I heard it—I knew I tended to view men reeking of alcohol with contempt—but Rosemary was tone deaf.

She looked across the table at me and shook her head. "Half a century and here we are. And not a damn bit of difference in you."

"You look the same," I lied, annoyed. When Rosemary and I worked together selling tourist insurance into Mexico, she'd annoyed me as much as intrigued me. The 'honky' label used to embarrass me, later amuse me—now I was indifferent. All the division and screaming from a hundred directions about race and cultural appropriation and political divides—the chasms gaped in front of the world and its people, and we were all going to fall in and go to hell. Because everybody now seemed to live for hate and on the social media attention that flared up to memorialize each new outrage.

My words stung; I could see it in the tightening of her lips and sudden tapping of her fingers on the table.

"Girl, I don't look the same at all!" She finished the drink she still had, and almost jerked the refresher out of the waiter's hand as he reached our table. "You don't live in California most of your life and come back the same!" She sloshed part of her drink on her face as she pointed to her nose. "New," she told me. "Like my hair, my boobs, and my teeth."

You couldn't have gotten all that here? I picked up my own drink, touched it to my lips, then set it back down.

"Were we ever friends?" I asked. "I mean, really? We worked together. We got along, mostly. But were we friends?"

She screwed up her face and drummed her fingers harder on the table.

"No," she said at last. "But I don't think that matters—neither of us had friends anyway. Not the way I remember."

"But here we are." I braved another sip of the strawberry flavored drink, but the alcohol stung.

Talk and bodies swirled around us, and the colored lights pulsing over the dance floor battered me.

"Rosemary Baby!" A beefy man in coveralls leaned in and kissed her on the cheek and forehead.

"Move it over," he ordered, and plopped down when she did. He looked across at me and frowned. "You look like Rosemary hogtied you and drug you here."

Great. Fifteen hundred miles from Georgia and a hillbilly like old man Newton shows up. I left home to get away from men like him.

"My friend Aggie," Rosemary told the man, and smiled. "You and me didn't work, but Aggie's all alone in the world." She shrugged, a gesture she apparently loved rolling out.

Hillbilly nodded and held out a hand. "Herb," he told me, nodding. "From Georgia once upon a time. Been chasing Rosemary Baby around the country for years." He shrugged. "But what can I say? Guess I'll never really catch her."

Rosemary elbowed him and grinned.

"Pleased to meet you," I muttered, not really looking into the bearded face. "But Rosemary lied. I'm not alone. I have six kids. My ex and I share custody."

A bushy eyebrow lifted. "How young are your kids?" He didn't seem irritated by the attempt to blow him off. Amused, maybe, which was annoying.

"The youngest is thirty-eight." I swallowed half the daiquiri and almost choked.

Rosemary hit Herb in the ribs again, a little harder. "I don't think you're impressing Abby, dude. Move it. I need to go pee. Keep my seat warm for me.

The uncomfortable silence pressed in as he sat back down and smiled at me. A smaller smile this time, not the exaggerated one a few moments ago. "Abby, I can leave. You clearly weren't here for me."

"Here for you?" I looked at him in confusion. "Why would I be? I just came because I thought I knew Rosemary. A lifetime ago, but—." I shrugged. "Turns out she isn't who I remembered."

"None of my business, but if you didn't come here to meet me—which is what she told me—why are you here?"

He genuinely seemed curious, and he wasn't as repulsive as when he'd been giving me the whole good old boy persona, so I answered. "I'm learning to wear red."

My answer confused him. He glanced at my quiet navy top. If he had the nerve to look under the table, he'd see navy slacks and black flats. He wasn't rude enough to do that, but I did see him glance at my ringless fingers a second time.

"Learning to wear red?" He lifted an eyebrow. "Is that some new thing or something? On some social platform or the other I'm not on yet?"

"Not a thing—not as far as I know. Just some idea from years ago about empowerment."

"You're not a red person?"

"No. Not empowered, either." A waiter passing by paused to offer us drinks. Rosemary was across the room. "Could I have a diet soda? Oh, and—would you like something, Herb?"

"Sure. I'll have the same."

The waiter nodded and hurried off.

"Are you really from Georgia? I couldn't help but notice that your accent changed a little when Rosemary left."

"Really? You've got a good ear. Yeah. Born and bred. But I flew the coop when I was eighteen and never went back, much to my family's dismay."

"I was going back," I offered, moving my glass around until a little sloshed over the top, then jerking my hand away in case I spilled the whole thing. "But...it never happened."

He nodded. "Let me guess. Marriage, kids—life torn up by the roots. Sometimes you still think you want to? Go back, I mean."

"Yeah. Sometimes. Mostly not."

Our brief communication dwindled, and we were both sitting in silence when Rosemary reappeared, her body still moving to the music. She shoved Herb playfully on the shoulder to move him over again, and perched on the outside edge of the bench.

"Have you two even spoken?" she asked

"Exchanged life stories and everything," he assured her, finishing a drink and pushing it aside with a face.

"What are you drinking?" Rosemary reached for his glass, sniffed it, then frowned at me.

"Really, girl? You got Herbie here on the wagon?"

Herb smiled at me. "Just joining the lady. That's what you brought me here for, right? Now get up and let this boy go home, okay?"

Rosemary sighed. "I'd say it was a waste, but I'm having fun." She stood up, and Herb slid out and bussed her on the cheek.

"Abby." He nodded, walked a step or two away and turned back. "I'll see you around," he told me, but didn't say when or how he would manage that.

"So whaddya think?" Rosemary leaned forward. "He's not Brad Pitt, but—"

"Is Brad Pitt still the guy to judge by?"

"Maybe not for your grandkids, no. But for women our age—sure. Him or Luis Miguel."

Mention of the Mexican pop singer made me smile. He'd been on all my friends' lips when he started topping the charts as a young teenager. Recently though, a former colleague and I had clashed over whether or not he owed his fans a face lift.

"I paid a lot to go see him," my co-worker protested. "He's an international superstar. He could afford to look better than he does."

"He's younger than both of us. And better looking than I am, certainly."

The colleague had spent a fortune on face sculpting and permanent lipstick and eyeliner, so I carefully ignored the fact that he looked better than both of us.

In the end, I quit arguing that appearances weren't something you owed to anyone else. Some days I wished I had that problem. Most days though I accepted my college roommate's description when she was pushing me to go out with a friend.

"You're not a dog," she said.

I had grinned. "Thanks, Becca. Really. When I cut my hair, mom said I looked like a jackass."

Becca had looked shocked, then sighed. "You could always come live with me, Abby. No strings. No rules."

I thanked her, but shook my head. "It's okay." I shot her another quick smile as I grabbed books for my literature class. "At least I'm moving up in the animal world."

Rosemary shifted across the table, drawing me back. "Hey, Honky, I'm still here."

I blinked.

"You don't mind that I call you that, right? Because I know I'm not supposed to, but—I just always did."

"I remember. In fact—you're in one of my poems. The one about southern girls and baseball games." I stood, smiling. "Thanks for tracking me down and bringing me here, Rosemary."

She got up too. "You know, if you didn't hit it off with Herb, there are other guys out there. And don't tell me you're not looking. We're all looking if we're alone. Hell, we're no better than guys. We look when we're with someone, too."

"Not me. I've never exactly blown anyone away—and I'm not looking for compliments."

"Still. Pull your boobs up. Let your hair down. Live, Abby. And I'll call you next Friday. Cause you're my new best friend."

Great. Just what I need. Someone else who wants to change me. Who wants me to wear red.

But like the well-behaved girl who had grown into a well-mannered, invisible woman, I nodded and walked away.

"Just pull my boobs up," I muttered, jerking again on the straps and plastic sliders stuck halfway up my bare back. The tug pulled the now wadded bra up to my neck, and the slider wouldn't move. I was choking myself with Perfect Bra Fixer and a bright red bra.

Maybe if I slid the darned plastic thingies higher up, the bra would loosen, and I wouldn't die. So I twisted my arm until it hurt, got a grip on the tiny plastic piece and tugged as hard as I could. Again, the various straps around my neck tightened and bit into my skin.

Apprehension became raw fear. I really couldn't free myself. Maybe if I could find scissors—

"Ma! Ma!" My daughter shrieked down the hall as she let herself in. "I got your text. What's wrong? Have you fallen? Did someone—"

She burst through the door, looked at me with my boobs sticking out and my bra with its brand-new Perfect Bra Fixers strangling me, and collapsed on the bed, shrieking with laughter instead of fear.

"Will you save my life, damn it? Please, Daniela?"

"Of course, Ma." She pushed herself off the bed, her face wet with tears. "I should take a picture." She wiped at her cheeks. "I haven't laughed this hard since—since maybe ever!" She looked at the contraption, caught the glides in her hands and slid them apart, loosening them. Everything fell off, and she grabbed a pillow and threw it at me.

"God, Ma! No one wants to see their mom naked." Daniela grabbed the robe lying across the foot of bed and threw it around me. "I'm not sure I'll ever get over this." She glanced at her phone. "I'm going to have to go. Sick kid."

Then she saw the dress lying across the pillows. Metallic red, shingled with sequins. "What is that—that—" Her usually impeccable English failed her, so she finished in Spanish "—*cochinada*?"

Like she didn't wear worse. "That "mess" is my dress, Daniela Marie."

"Your dress? To wear where? You wouldn't have let me wear that when I was eighteen! Besides, you don't wear red—you have never worn red. And—where would you wear something that short and tight?"

"To dinner. With a friend. And you know what? I don't want or need to be told by my daughter what I can do, with whom, or—"

"You're going out with someone? Like—a date?"

"Again—I don't need your permission—"

"Did you meet someone on Craig's List or something? I can't believe—you swore you'd never go out. That you wanted to stay at home and not answer to anyone—"

"Yet here I am, answering to you."

The bitterness and defeat piercing me must have registered.

"Ma," she said, "look, if you're going out with someone—you should at least let us know. Just—there are so many creeps out there these days. What if he's some pervert trying to con you out of money or something? What if he's violent?"

"What if I'm older, not stupider, and the only bad relationship I was ever in was with—"

Even in my anger, I couldn't finish. However little I had mattered to him, my husband had been devoted to his kids.

"You never wore red," Daniela said stubbornly. "Never." She sighed and shrugged. "I just pray you're not being stupid." She kissed me on the forehead as if I were the child. "Do what you want. You will anyway."

And then she was gone, but her words hung in the sudden silence of the room. I'd thrown those exact words at her when she'd walked out the door to move in with her boyfriend.

I sighed and sat down on the bed. They'd been married ten years now. Maybe her judgement was better than mine.

My phone buzzed with a text notification. I dug it out from under the dress.

Rosemary: Hey, Honky. Go out with me to dinner?

I keyed in the letters carefully, still not fluent with texting. "Sorry," I. read as I typed. Then I stopped. *I'm not sorry.* I erased the apology and typed *No*.

The red dress lay across the bed.

When Herb rang my doorbell two hours later, I opened the door only as far as the security chain allowed and peered out at him.

He looked confused. "Am I early? We were going out to dinner..." He smiled. "You were going to wear that red dress you told me about."

"You're not early, Herb. But you need to know this—I don't wear red." I took the chain off and pulled the door a little wider. "I wear gray a lot, or dark blue or dark green. I don't wear heels, and I really don't like going out much."

He lifted his eyebrows. "Okay." He looked away for a moment, then back at me. I couldn't tell if he wanted to laugh, curse, or run. "Just out of curiosity—why the sudden change?"

"Sudden change, Herb? This is me. It's who I always was."

"But not who you wanted to be yesterday." He held up his phone. "We texted all night about that red dress."

"Yeah, well—I had a near death experience. Everything's clearer. If you're okay with sweatpants and gray, come on in."

He didn't say anything, just followed me through the house.

Hours later, when the gray came off and the killer bra fell to the floor, I heard him laugh softly.

"Well, damn, girl—I guess you learned to wear red after all

***

The Years Before

Putting together this collection of some of my writing has been a rewarding trip. There's more—on my old HP baby, on this laptop, on the computer that died and took so much writing and all the pictures of my children with it. But the reason for that was the realization that I've become the caricature of me on the cover—an old woman with white hair trying to fend off her ghosts.

Along with a lifelong passion to write is an almost as strong need to keep up with the news, and the internet has made that ridiculously easy and addictive.

Unfortunately, the news today is horrific, and just when you think the world can't move closer to total destruction than ever—it does. And mixed in with nuclear warfare, famines, and hatred are far too many stories about people abusing others for little or no reason—and the worst crime conceivable to me, abusing children, and receiving little to no punishment for it.

The truth is that my past abuse haunts me, and I want nothing more than to lay it aside for good. But to quote from Shakespeare's Hamlet, "there lies the rub." My daughters, who have been my conscience since they were way too young to bear that burden, are split. One believes being open about it will help, the other that I should just get on with my life. The truth is that I have "gotten on with my life," but the memories and ghosts have, too—and they still taunt me. And there are episodes so vile and painful that they won't see the light of day, ever. Those are the ones I chase around in the darkness, trying to destroy with a sword of reason that never seems to work. I have six surviving siblings, but I will only mention Stephanie, who has spoken and written about our abuse, and who let me get through life by clinging to her.

I grew up calling Stephanie "Steve," as my father did. That alone should make me quit and call her "Steph," as so many others do, but when we were kids—she didn't have another name. She's three years older than me, and was a fearless little girl who has grown into a woman of endless courage and selflessness.

I'm not sure where our memories begin, because there was so much fluidity in our childhoods. I suppose I should have become used to moves, separations, and always wondering "now what?", but I always hated how temporary everything seemed. She must have been there in California, because she remembers Roy Rogers' yacht, too.

But we weren't always there. At some point, my father took Steve and his mother and moved to Texas. My mom took me and my little brother Greg to Texas on a train. (The only thing I remember from the train ride was that my pet locust, Lucky, jumped in the train's heater and burned to death, so I cried from CA to Texas.)

Steve and I were reunited in Texas, where she had been born. She was thrilled to be back in TX, and I'm sure I annoyed the heck out of her—I hated everything. The half-roofed log cabin my father built, the mosquitoes, eating outside day and night—I blamed the state, rather than my father's poor planning.

Abruptly, though—my father disappeared, and he took his mother and Stephanie with him. I didn't know then, but it became one of the many knives in my heart when later, Stephanie shared her suspicions about why they hid out in the Florida Everglades.

Over the next several years there were constant moves, and I never felt at home until we arrived in Georgia. To this day, I'm a little surprised I never made it back to the state I thought I loved.

At six, no child should be wonder why they are unloved, or face displays of child sexual abuse, even if they don't know what they are seeing. My reaction to the time Dad spent "saying goodnight" to Steve was anger—and hurt feelings. I wondered why he didn't want anything to do with me—the bliss of innocence, which would end soon enough.

For the first time, I resented Steve—we still got along, and she still was the one person I'd follow anywhere, but I was jealous of all the attention she got that I didn't.

I complained to Mom, and was scolded for being jealous and selfish. After all, she told me, "She's older. So, he's known her longer, and there's more she can do."

She must have told him, though, because not long after that, after he said goodnight to Stephanie, he came and sat down on my bed, which he never did.

He said something about how grownup I was (I was 7) and began massaging me. The feeling was weird, but we grew up being told "Don't speak until you're spoken to." I had been a stickler for rules all my life, because Stephanie had never been, and was always in trouble. But when his hand went under my pajama bottoms, I recoiled and gasped.

At the same time, my mom called him, and he jerked away and stood up. "Coming. The girls were just having trouble sleeping. You shouldn't let them watch all those scary things—"

He walked out, and I just laid awake a long time feeling sick, but not knowing why. I wanted to ask Stephanie, but I felt ashamed. What if she thought I was stupid, not knowing?

The insomnia began when I was very young, and I still don't sleep well. I expect knowing there really are monsters in the dark who sneak into rooms is why even now my lights are always on, and my peak hours to sleep are from 9am to 11.

***

A LETTER AND GONE WITH THE WIND

There's truth in the cliché that children are resilient. Even with the constant abuse in our lives, Steve and I had fun. We'd been given a horse and pony—as bribes, I expect, but why didn't become as important as the escape they provided.

Our house was located at the intersection of two red clay roads. We had friends up the hill, and in the other direction my best childhood friend and her pony, and her brother. Her brother was good-looking, Stephanie's age, and had a horse, at least for a short time. At the same time, my father's shift at Lockheed changed—so he usually wasn't there when we came home, and we could go to bed not worrying about him coming in on the pretense of saying goodnight.

Those had to be the best days of our childhood. Mom also had an overnight shift—she was the librarian for the Atlanta area newspaper—and she slept days. We were basically unsupervised—and probably as safe and as happy as we had ever been. We were adventurous, but not "wild," and we could do anything we wanted with her approval so long as we were home by twilight.

Ironically, I think now the one time we were safe was when we were out among strangers. They didn't have horses, but our best friends were the twins up the hill from us, with the annoying baby brother who happened to be our brother's age. Given our excursions into Douglasville by ourselves, asking strangers if they had Coke bottles we could return—just running on our own lives, Stephanie and I were safer than we'd ever been. And happier.

Then my mom and dad asked for day shift "to be home more," and all the old horrors began again. I felt guilty, because I would offer to get groceries and run errands with Mom—she had to drive in to Marietta or Smyrna, and would be gone hours—and I knew what was happening at home.

The abuse would continue for years, especially for Stephanie.

We moved to Greenville, a couple hours drive from Douglasville, and Mom and Dad continued working. The lengthy drive meant they were home less often—which was wonderful. Unfortunately, the abuse didn't stop. In desperation—and because I wrote—I wrote a letter to *Dear Abby*.

I slaved over the letter, trying to explain my feelings without being gross, to shield Mom by saying she didn't know, and I didn't want to tell her—I spent so long writing that letter. I carried it around in my pocket, just needing an envelope and stamp.

She washed the clothes. I hadn't thought about that, and I'd forgotten to hide the letter. But when she found it—she shared it with *him*.

I suppose she thought showing it to my father was the right thing to do. I still find it hard to blame her for any of her actions or inaction.

He took me with him to work—only, he didn't go in to work. I thought he would kill me. He beat me, berated me, called me all the names I learned too early, "whore," and "bitch," and "cunt." He told me I'd been "asking for it" since I was six months old, and I "used to rub against him and ask for it" even then. I would have been okay if he'd left me there in the woods by that deserted house to die.

He took me back to "apologize" to Mom, and make her believe it was just me wanting to impress someone with my writing, and I'd been too real.

With all I went through, I remember my mom's face most—she had tears in her eyes, and when I stammered through just wanting to see if I could get my letter published, I don't think she knew what to do. She nodded once, and said "okay," and everything stopped there. Except the abuse.

Dad had a photo lab at the house in Douglasville. He was a professional photographer, and often was hired for weddings, parties or horse shows—all sorts of events that needed high quality photos.

I always wanted to be good with a camera, and he used that as a pretext one night, saying he needed help, and Stephanie had homework.

I felt worth something again, finally—his photography was important to him, and you had to mix the chemicals to develop them very carefully. He had asked Stephanie for help, and my oldest brother, but never me.

As naïve as always at the time, I didn't know he had no intention of developing photos. The photography lab was the farthest room from the door in an aluminum building with stalls for the horses. There were a dark room with the red "working" light, a lock on the main door, and a mattress on the floor. There was also a working shower in the lab in case of chemical spills on the skin.

He stretched out on the mattress and lit a cigarette, telling me to relax. He wouldn't let me go visit the ponies. When he finished smoking, he said he didn't really have any photos, but we hadn't had any time together. He tore my clothes off when I just sat like a rock, raped me brutally, then told me to go into shower and go back to the house later.

As usual, I did what he said, but first I went to Smokey's stall, sat down with him, and wept.

I don't know how much later they sent Greg for me, but I got back to a dark house. Greg said Mom and Dad were driving into work early and were angry I'd been gone so long. I just stared at him and wondered if he could tell what had happened—the feeling of dirtiness didn't leave after I showered.

I was in the fourth grade that year, finally had made friends at school, and was looking forward to the arrival of the re-release of *Gone With the Wind* at the Fox Theatre in downtown Atlanta. Stephanie stayed home with my two youngest brothers, and the rest of us rode into Atlanta for the movie.

I didn't really want to go. I knew that Mr. Butler, the pony, would die, and the daughter, too, and I hated going into Atlanta. But I had to go.

On the way home, just leaving the brightest lights of Atlanta, there was a terrifying orange glow lighting up the horizon in our direction.

Someone said something about a terrible fire, and I asked, "What if it's our house?" My parents scolded me for always believing the worst, and I scrunched down in my seat and didn't speak. But I knew the house was ours.

Making the last turn and coming on a scene with multiple fire engines, police, news cameras and onlookers was sickening. Not knowing if Stephanie and my brothers were alive was terrifying.

Stephanie had burns on her hands, but the two boys were fine. Mom was distraught—her 19-year-old Siamese Pan and her 20-year-old Persian were dead. She'd often told us they were with her before she even met our father. There had been a library with hundreds of books—three walls of them—and the original vinyl records from numerous artists, because my father had been a sound engineer.

Neighbors pitched in as they do in much of the south, finding places for us to stay, bringing food and personal items—and none of us knew at the time the fire's true story.

My father dealt with the insurance company and remarkably—or suspiciously fast, we were on our way to Greenville, Georgia to live in a rundown antebellum on what had once been a small plantation.

If events hadn't driven me crazy, that place did. There was no plumbing in the house, no water, and for the first few days, no electricity. The house had large rooms downstairs that the fireplaces didn't warm, and a staircase to the upper floor with three or four rooms, no heat, and a balcony. There were holes between the roof and the walls, and bats flew in. So, with nothing else to do really, Stephanie and

I—but mostly my sis—caught bats and put them in a large wire cage. We got up to 39 before Mom found them and made us turn them loose.

Our moving in inconvenienced the copperheads that lived happily along and under the side porch, and I lived in fear of being bitten, especially since we had to trek to the outhouse that way.

We discovered the Civil War cemetery the next day, and quickly heard—and saw—that the former owner's son, a high school baseball player, had been killed in a game, and visited the cemetery most nights. Old jeans, tee shirt and baseball cap—he appeared their often, and the voices in the pecan grove drove me crazy.

Our school was okay, but the superintendent's daughter was in my grade. I'm not saying she was valedictorian because of her father—she was pretty, smart, and I didn't have problems with her. Her mother, my homeroom teacher in 5th grade, hated me. But to be honest, I would have only scraped by in algebra no matter who taught it, and I never blamed teachers.

In English class one day, I was giving a book report. The story had been assigned, and was a horrible story—these kids on a chicken farm lost both their parents at the same time. Speaking in front of others never bothered me, but I fell apart, aware that my period was unusually heavy, and unless I got out of the room—they called my parents when I passed out, and when I came to, I was being rushed to a hospital in Atlanta.

I didn't remember the trip, or much else. My mother was there first, telling me not to worry, that there was an emergency alert for O-blood all over Atlanta. Groggy and cold, I didn't understand that at first. Later my father came and hung around. I wished my mom were there instead.

He stood by my bed, leaned over me, and told me if they asked me what happened, I should say that I was standing up on Smokey and fell on the saddle horn. My first thought was that I couldn't, because they might shoot Smokey. Then the s.o.b. put his hand under the cover and groped me until a nurse came in.

Nothing that happened when I was in the hospital really registered with me. But now, I wonder why nobody said anything. No one asked me, or as far as I know my parents, about what happened. Honestly, I might not have known what to say. But I can't believe doctors bought the saddle horn excuse.

I heard a nurse and doctor talking in the hall early on, and I think the nurse was petitioning him to call the police, but that never happened. And, if my father had been in the room—I probably would have said what I was told to. You couldn't defy him, then or ever.

When I heard we were moving again—for the first time in my life I was happy. Except—we were going back to Texas.

***

Texas X 2

Supposedly, my father had been transferred to Lockheed in SanAntonio. As far as I know, he didn't work once he came back, although I could be wrong. I believe Mom found a job at one of the papers as a librarian, but even that is foggy. No offense to Stephanie or anyone else, but I hated the Hill Country. That my mom and dad lived in an old camper and were building a house that had neither working plumbing nor running water when I was there didn't appeal to me, either.

The house was near Pipe Creek, which at the time was a tiny town with a handful of folks. There were no large stores you could get to on foot, just twisted caliche roads and a lot of goats. My impression of Texas deteriorated, and I hadn't liked the falling on my head part the first time around.

One day, Steve encouraged me to walk with her to the one little store we knew of. She had a dollar, and we were going to share a Coke.

Coke was our magic word at the time.

On the way, she confided in me that she'd met a guy at a place where she'd painted a sign and that he mentioned there were other jobs available. Immediately I knew that the unspoken part of her conversation was that she liked the guy. What seemed an inconsequential meeting would change both our lives—and Willie Nelson would unknowingly play a part, too.

My father hated country music, so it surprised me when he took my mother, Stephanie and me to a bar in nearby Helotes to see Willie Nelson. The place appalled me—so many people crowded in, everyone smoking and drinking—and all these women handing Willie Nelson cups with numbers and flirting with him as if he were good looking or could sing.

A tall, blond young man approached our table, smiling. Stephanie smiled, too, and I realized this was the guy she wanted me to meet.

But here? Dad's glare was exactly what I expected, and part of me wanted to crawl away through the crowded bar and escape whatever unpleasantness was about to erupt.

The guy introduced himself as Army, Mom introduced dad as Navy, and everyone stared awkwardly at each other, until Stephanie thanked him for helping her get the sign straight. He shrugged. "Plywood signs are a pain, and they're too heavy for one person. Let me know if you need help with one again."

Maybe picking up on Dad's frown, he excused himself. Steve watched him, smiling, until the door closed behind him, then turned back to us. "He's the greatest isn't he?"

Dad ignored her, I nodded slightly enough I hoped only Stephanie noticed, and Mom beamed. "What a sweet young man," she said. "I hope we see him again sometime."

Mom and Dad slept in the isolated camper, leaving the long, unlit house with the cold-water faucets for the six of us children. We routinely tripped over each other, walked in on each other in the bathroom, since there were no doors, just verbal warnings to protect privacy—but if anyone complained, I never heard it.

Until Steve managed to get my attention and get me to go outside. She was building a rock path outside, finding flat rocks and putting them together to lead toward the camper. I admired her work—the rocks were heavy, the bags of cement she carried around weighed a ton—and still she sang and worked like one of Snow White's dwarves.

She dropped the rock she was holding, and jerked her head in the direction of the road leading into what was quickly becoming a neighborhood in the formerly empty wilderness. "Walk with me," she said, and I braced myself for what I expected to be bad news for me, and likely dangerous to boot.

"I really like Larry," she announced, but I already knew that. "He wants to ask Dad if we can date, but—"

"Yeah."

"Well, I think I'm leaving home.'"

"Leaving home?" I stopped in the caliche road, and she dragged me to the side as a pickup barreled past, blasting its horn. "You can't do that—"

"I'm an adult. I have a job. Larry and I might marry, we don't know. But I'm not staying home with *him* anymore." She gestured toward our house.

"There's a dude ranch not far from here. They need someone. I met the old couple who own it. You can stay there, and they'll pay you and they divide tips."

I had stopped listening after 'dude ranch'. "They'll have horses! I'll be able to ride again!"

We'd made so many plans together as kids, always together, never considering we might wind up on separate roads—but this was the beginning of goodbye.

The elderly owner of the place looked me over, and told me my job would mostly be to clean cabins and help during dinners. Occasionally there were ranch activities that would require extra hours. She didn't pay overtime, but tips were good for trail rides and cookouts. She would like me to start in the morning at 8.

Steve had waited outside to see if I needed one last ride home. We didn't talk at all. I collected the few clothes I owned and promised Mom I'd visit her whenever I could get home for a few hours. My younger siblings were in school, and not waiting to say goodbye hurt. But knowing I'd never have to suffer my father's assaults again made it worthwhile.

The next morning, after a night I spent in a cavernous unused cabin next to the laundry tower, I walked in through the front door. No one told me what door to use, and I figured at least the owner would know who I was. As I approached the kitchen, a man around my age and looked out the window and winked.

In almost 18 years, that hadn't happened. Maybe Texas would be better this time around.

Old Folks, Old Ways

The first person I met when I walked into the kitchen was the good-looking guy who had been washing dishes, and was running them through the sterilizing machine when I went in. He had dark, wavy hair, brown eyes, and dark skin, and wore a long-sleeved western shirt, jeans, and boots. He looked dressed to ride, and spoke virtually no English. I thought maybe he finished dishes then went out to lead the trail rides advertised in brochures about the ranch. But when I came in, he disappeared behind the center food prep area, and the cook came over to introduce herself.

She was short, heavy, and had white hair pulled back severely into a bun, covered by a net. When she saw me, she slapped her hips with such force I thought it probably hurt. "Well, damn it to hell!" she muttered, then went back to the stoves and began pulling out trays of biscuits.

"She Casey," a second man told me, smiling at me. "I Lolo, I speak a little English—" He held up a hand, demonstrating "a little" with his forefinger and thumb, "and I am here 12 years. *Mi compadre Cruz*"—he pointed at the dishwasher, now chopping up vegetables on the other side of the island, "he come with me many years now."

Casey slapped her hips again and cussed.

"She do that much," Lolo offered, "but she *una buena persona.*"

I didn't speak Spanish, was intimidated by being told sometimes I'd be serving a hundred people after cleaning all the cabins, and unless the gruff old wrangler Noe ever felt like giving other staff members a break, I'd never ride one of the forty horses. But I could pet them, hug them, and choose my favorites. All in all, I decided I loved the working life, as long as it was on a dude ranch.

Bobbie, the 80-year-old owner, still lead the trail rides herself occasionally . We'd go through some of the hills on the ranch, cross an arroyo, and then she'd stop at the top of one of the flatter hills and launch into an interesting, but undoubtedly politically incorrect, account of her family and the ranch's early history.

Her parents bought the land, angering other settlers and Native American tribes in the area. She called them "Indians," and I don't know whether "politically correct" has caught up with the owners of the area ranches yet or not. Back then, it hadn't.

She would point out which stunted bush or dried weed was what, but I really didn't remember any of that. She rode a docile old mare named Petunia, and I was stuck, when I was invited to ride, on a sweet, placid bay named Rex. Sometimes Cruz went with us if Noe didn't, and he always chose the gelding I would have, Comanche. The bright chestnut was spirited and gorgeous. In the corral, he and I were good friends. But Bobbie doubted that I'd ever had horses and just didn't want to lose an employee who could clean rooms, serve meals, and take her place at the desk when she left for her nap and to check up on her ailing husband. There were days I felt more like one of the family members than an employee.

I worked hard, and there were frustrations, but I came to love the dude ranch. And working day after day with Cruz, finding out his mother had recently passed away from cancer, that at eight years he would compete in boxing matches against older opponents to help support his family—I fell in love with Cruz.

I knew better. If nothing else, I found out that when Stephanie left Bandera with her new husband, somebody in the FBI did look into him, and they were stopped on several occasions. None of the stops were valid, and finally they stopped, but Dad's boasts about knowing people were apparently true. I would have done well to understand the danger I was in, because relationships rarely are secret in small towns.

After a few months, Cruz began sneaking out of the wash tower, a small version of a lighthouse, and spending the night with me. I was terrified that the boss would find out, but I also loved Cruz. He argued with me and wanted to tell her about our relationship, but if my father found out, I knew our lives would be in danger.

Cruz proposed to me. He wanted to marry me, he said, and he wanted to ask my father for my hand. He told me that if my father knew he wanted us to marry, then he would agree. His innocence touched me, but I knew better.

We outed ourselves to our boss first, who said if we were going to be together, she didn't want to be attacked by angry parents or have someone call the police or border patrol. She called my father and asked him to come in, then told Cruz and me to join them. Haltingly, Cruz said he loved me and wanted to marry him.

My father never said a word. He got up and walked out without looking at any of us.

On March 1st, 1974, Cruz and I went to the Bandera Courthouse to marry. He wore a white shirt, jeans, boots, and his black. My only dress was navy blue, and I wore my work sneakers. My sister Stephanie was there for us. The county clerk refused to marry us. She didn't give us a reason, but she told her co-workers—loudly—she "wouldn't marry a wetback and white trash."

Her outburst brought a judge out of his office, and when I told him why we were there, he took us into his little office and married us himself. After the vows, he asked us to promise never to divorce without speaking to him first. We kept that promise; we were married until Cruz passed away 43 years later.

On March 1st, 1974, I was at the Kerrville Hospital waiting for the birth of our son. Cruz had not come; we had initiated his immigration papers, but didn't want to have anything complicate the process. At the time, we were told the process would take at least 12 years.

I have virtually no memory of the experience except that it took forever, and I didn't see Cruzito for several hours. When a nurse finally brought him to me, she scolded me. "Why did you lie to us about not having other children?" she asked. "We were worried about complications."

Only years later, even though I'd heard about the need for Rhogam if you were O- and pregnant with a baby with a different blood type did I realize—Cruzito wasn't my first. At 9, I miscarried a baby—and doctors did nothing about it.

I am a believer in mandatory reporters, although I know that many teachers worry about the possible consequences of having to do so. But not making a report if a reasonable belief of the abuse exists—that feels like betraying a child to me.

Stiffer sentences for child abusers should also be adopted. I recently saw a custodial parent who abused a child received a sentence of two months. That's not a joke; it's an insult, and a crime itself.

The bad dreams and darkness have gone for me—but for much of my life, they were there. I found myself moving through darkness, by myself I thought. Now the issue has become so prevalent that the response too often these days is, "oh, another me, too story?" followed by a yawn.

Children deserve better.

***